PERFECTLY FREE

AN AMARYLLIS/MIDAS CROSSOVER

MIDAS SERIES
BOOK 6

TRACEY JERALD

Copyright © 2022 by Tracey Jerald

ISBN: 978-1-959299-03-5 (eBook)

ISBN: 978-1-959299-16-5 (Paperback)

ISBN: 978-1-959299-14-1 (Alternate Cover Paperback)

Library of Congress Control Number: TBD

Tracey Jerald

101 Marketside Avenue, Suite 404-205

Ponte Vedra, FL, 3208

https://www.traceyjerald.com

Editor: Melissa Borucki

Proof Edits: Holly Malgieri (https://www.facebook.com/HollysRedHotReviews/)

Cover Design by Tugboat Design (https://www.tugboatdesign.net/)

Photo Credit: Wander Aguiar Model: Robbin

PR & Marketing: Linda Russell - Foreword PR (https://www.forewordpr.com)

DEDICATION

To Holly.

It's not just because you're my twin, though that part rocks.

It's also because you understand Andy Pettitte's fills out pinstripes better than any man in baseball history.

Love you forever.

PLAYLIST

ABBA: "Dancing Queen"
The Rolling Stones: "Honky Tonk Woman"
Dua Lipa, DaBaby: "Levitating"
Imagine Dragons: "Bones"
Amanda Marshall: "Birmingham"
Boston: "Peace of Mind"
ZZ Top: "Gimme All Your Lovin' "
'38 Special: "Hold On Loosely"
'38 Special: "Caught Up In You"
Pink Floyd: "Another Brick In the Wall"
Jack Wagner: "All I Need"
Billy Joel: "Shameless"
Foreigner: "I Want To Know What Love Is"
Scarlet: "Independent Love Song"
Enya: "Caribbean Blue"
Lady Gaga: "Paparazzi"
The Chainsmokers, Coldplay: "Something Just Like This"
Madonna: "Ghosttown"
Taylor Swift: "All Too Well"
Toby Lightman: "Breathe In"

TRACEY JERALD

ALSO BY TRACEY JERALD

MIDAS SERIES

Perfect Proposal

Perfect Assumption

Perfect Composition

Perfect Order

Perfect Satisfaction

Perfectly Free (A Midas/Amaryllis Crossover)

Perfect Pitch (coming Summer 2023)

Amaryllis Series

Free to Dream

Free to Run

Free to Rejoice

Free to Breathe

Free to Believe

Free to Live

Free to Dance

Free to Wish

Free to Protect

Free to Reunite

Perfectly Free (An Amaryllis/Midas Crossover)

Devotion Series

Ripple Effect

Flood Tide

Glacier Adventure Series

Return by Air

Return by Land

Return by Sea

Standalones

Close Match

Go to https://www.traceyjerald.com/ for all buy links!

THE MIDAS TOUCH

In Greek mythology, Midas, wandering one day in his garden, came across the wise satyr Silenus, who was rather the worse for wear. Midas treated him kindly and returned him to his great companion, the god Dionysus

In return for this, Dionysus granted Midas a wish. The king, not realizing the repercussions of his decision, chose to be given the magical ability to turn any object he touched into solid gold. Simple things, everyday things, Midas took for granted were instantly transformed by his touch into solid gold.

The full consequences of this gift soon became evident. At the barest touch, flowers, fruit, and water turned to gold. Food took on a metallic taste the moment it brushed his lips. Midas became sick of this world he surrounded himself with and sought to relieve himself of it.

Those finding themselves burdened with an abundance of perfection gifted to them by the gods often seek relief to reverse their fortune.

Except when that gift is love. Then, it is a treasure of unfathomable value.

And it's absolutely something you never want to rid yourself of.

THE LEGEND OF AMARYLLIS

THERE ARE VARIATIONS REGARDING THE LEGEND OF HOW amaryllis flowers came to be. Generally, the tale is told like this:

Amaryllis, a shy nymph, fell deeply in love with Alteo, a shepherd with great strength and beauty, but her love was not returned. He was too obsessed with his gardens to pay much attention to her.

Amaryllis hoped to win Alteo over by giving him the one thing he wanted most, a flower so unique it had never existed in the world before. She sought advice from the oracle Delphi and carefully followed his instructions. She dressed in white, and for thirty nights, appeared on Alteo's doorstep, piercing her heart with a golden arrow.

When Alteo finally opened his eyes to what was before him, he saw only a striking crimson flower that sprung from the blood of Amaryllis's heart.

It's not surprising the amaryllis has come to be the symbol of pride, determination, and radiant beauty. What's also not surprising is somehow, someway, we all bleed a little bit while we're falling in love.

AUTHOR'S NOTE

Dear Reader,

If you've read the Amaryllis Series or the Midas Series, thank you for loving Danielle Madison and Brendan Blake as much as I do. If this is your first book of mine, I'm so excited to introduce you to them.

I appreciate your eagerness for their story as they've been a part of my life since Brendan was first mentioned in Amaryllis by Corinna Freeman. That said, Danielle and Brendan's story could not be told before now. Their story involves several other individuals from both the Amaryllis and Midas Series.

If you have yet to read Perfect Satisfaction (Midas Series, book 5), there may be parts of that book that some could construe as spoilers, which I could not avoid. While I enjoyed bringing some of your favorite characters into never before viewed material, I tried to divert your attention from other book's critical plot points. One of the subplots of Perfect

Satisfaction was crucial to how Danielle and Brendan evolved as a couple.

It also was the catalyst for how I wove Amaryllis and Midas together.

The first time they met, Brendan Blake stormed into Danielle Madison's life. From that moment on, nothing was the same for either of these characters.

No, it wasn't fables or myths that drove this particular story, though I touch on both. It was simply the love of two people who made me realize I was Perfectly Free to weave their story because my heart said it was the right thing to do.

Danielle and Brendan are legends in their own right. She is a world-renowned supermodel and he an up-and-coming country music star at a time when amaryllises are just starting to bloom and being showered with riches hasn't jaded anyone.

Yet.

I hope you enjoy reading the beginning of both series.

XOXO,
Tracey Jerald

CHAPTER ONE

Danielle

PRESENT DAY

THE BREEZE OFF THE ATLANTIC OCEAN OFFERS A REPRIEVE FROM the early morning sun caressing my skin. There's nothing but miles of sand and crashing waves in front of me. It's my oasis in a world of sheer chaos stirring at this very moment at my back.

Not that I would have it any other way.

Tilting my head, I can just pick out the sounds of a drum kit being whaled on with no consideration to the other people sleeping in the multistory residence. My smile is as vast as my family. Amused, I give voice to my thoughts. "If there's one thing I've learned, it's that musical genius waits for nothing—not even a respectable time of day."

That's when I feel him. It's the same shock of electricity that struck a bolt of awareness down my back the first time we intersected at a party over twenty years and three children ago. My breath quickens, knowing he's nearby.

Anticipating his touch.

I curl my toes in the still damp sand behind the beach house we've opened to our closest family and friends to celebrate our twentieth anniversary as a couple.

From the moment we met, he stormed into my life—a force I was desperately grateful for. Although we had a rocky start, it didn't take either of us long for us to realize we were more free to be ourselves together than apart. My heart was lost without some part of him near— whether just a nightly call, a quick visit at one of his shows, or him appearing on the red carpet for one of my events.

I knew I would never be the same if things didn't work out between us. "I was right."

One night, my soul shattered because fate decreed I needed to know him for the man he was, not the man he pretended to be. A man forced to hide behind a mask in order to have the right to love me.

What a fool. I loved him more for what he kept hidden in shadow than what shone in the spotlight.

After he set aside the scars of his youth and trusted what I told him to be true—that my love would wrap around as many people as he needed it to —he knew I was in this relationship for the long haul.

Laughter explodes from the back deck before I hear my cousin's wife yell, "Jake! If you throw me in the pool, you will regret it!"

With a grin, I think about how one curly-haired blond will exact revenge on my cousin if he acts on tossing his wife into the water.

That's when I hear footfalls on the stairs. And I wait.

I feel him coming. Soon, he'll wrap me in his strong arms again, my own heaven on earth. My eyes drift shut with anticipation.

Love was never the issue between Brendan and me. The secrets of his past threatened our relationship when at its most vulnerable point. And insecurity fueled by my own inexperience and the press, I admit to myself as brutally honest now as I was then.

Deep down to the depths of my soul, I know Brendan Blake will love me until we're both nothing more than vague memories to the people who spent hours speculating about how we should never have made it.

The sand depresses behind me. The zing of awareness becomes a tidal wave of emotions as Brendan slips his arms around me. He pulls me back against his jean-clad legs to rest against his hair-roughened chest. Chin propped against my shoulder, he turns his head to the side and brushes his lips against the column of my neck before murmuring, "Happy anniversary, Dancing Queen."

I slightly twist so I can capture his lips in a languid kiss. "Happy anniversary, Honky Tonk."

His mouth rests against mine when he whispers, "Have I ever said thank you?"

Jerking back, I ask, "For what?"

"For loving me. For never giving up on me. And above all, accepting all of us when you never had to."

Love and anger whip through me in equal measure. I spin around in the sand until I can straddle his hips. My arms looping over his broad shoulders. "First, loving you hasn't always been easy, but it has always—always—been worth it."

A ray of sun illuminates the smile that's mine alone—not the one seen by millions of fans all over the world. "Danielle . . .," he begins.

"Second, we never gave up on each other. We saved each other." I cup his jaw, feeling the rasp of his unshaved skin against the palm of my hand. "Or do you not remember how the night we met?"

His head drops to my chest. "I'll never forget."

A dark night. Violent fear. And a man with a lazy drawl and lethal smile who stormed in to rescue someone he didn't know. What neither of us realized was that one instant would cause an avalanche of more secrets to be exposed than any tabloid could dare dream. He murmurs, "And to think, I used to just be annoyed by the fact they wrote about my fans not liking you."

The crashing of the ocean behind us absorbed the sound of my laughter. I tease, "Now look at what they get to write about? And who gets to write about it?" There's so much more fuel for the gossip fodder now than whether I was at every one of his shows—and if not, why? We exchange a devilish smile when we both pick out a particular voice giving her husband an earful before there's a distinct yelp followed by a massive splash.

Score one for Sula. Her husband must have written something truly outrageous, I think, with a touch of admiration knowing Sula only gives Arek a hard time when he mentions family in his news magazine. Then a second splash sounds, and Brendan and I shake with laughter knowing she's likely followed her husband into the pool.

Back then, while the planet followed the paparazzi alerts about whether we—me, at the time, the world's most famous supermodel and him, country's hottest musician—would tie the knot, I thought I knew better. Brendan was adamant he would never get married. I told myself I could have lived with that if the piece of paper was the only obstacle to our happily ever after.

That wasn't the reason he almost lost me.

I almost ran away because of the one thing I couldn't stand from the man I loved.

Lies.

Brendan was determined to protect the people who cracked through the stronghold he'd built around his soul. I ran away to protect what I had left of mine.

In the end, confronting the lies brought us together.

"We," I emphasize, "never gave up."

His voice is tender when he says, "Because when you tried to, I refused to let you go."

I lean back in his arms. "Because you always stormed back into my life. Your choice. No giving me back now."

He hauls me to his chest before toppling us both in the sand. Rolling me to my back, he murmurs, "Like I'd ever give back the best part of my life. I love you, Danielle. Now. Always."

As he leans down to capture my lips, my mind drifts back to our beginning, which ultimately led to him confessing everything right here in this very spot.

Thank God I didn't have to let him go because he finally told me everything.

CHAPTER TWO

Danielle

Honky-Tonk Hunk, Brendan Blake, was seen leaving the *Incandesce* party with none other than supermodel, Danielle Madison. No two celebrities on the planet sparkle as much as these two when snapped by a camera.

—New York Entertainment

TWENTY-ONE YEARS AGO

"I SWEAR IF YOU DON'T GET YOUR HANDS OFF ME, I'LL MAKE YOU regret it." I reach behind me and forcefully dig my nails into the hands of the photographer who followed me onto the balcony.

"Aww, come on, Danielle. S'ou soo know s'ou s'want shis," Wallis slurs. He's consumed so much alcohol, his breath might spark a fire is he gets too close to a flame.

"Yeah. I want you groping me even less now than I wanted you touching me on set." I struggle to get away as his arm bands tighter around me. I shout, "That wasn't an invitation, you asshole!"

"I swaw s'way you slooked at s'me," he counters as he pushes me away from the light of the party into the darkest corner.

Panic causes a greasy, oily feeling to well up in my stomach. Immediately, I use all my strength to whale on the grizzly-like man. Recalling one of the self-defense maneuvers my cousin Jake taught me, I twist the large jewel on my right ring finger inside my hand before slapping the bastard across his gluttonous face.

Blood trickles down his cheek as he gapes at me incredulously.

I edge to the side carefully. "I'm sorry. You just wouldn't—"

I'm not given leave to finish my sentence before he slams me against the wall full force, shouting, "God damn prick tease!"

Even as fear and terror fight to take over what's left of my mind, I desperately hang on to a shred of sanity. *This can't be happening.* "Help! Someone, please help me."

With a single meaty paw, he tears the front of one side of my dress from its strap. I stop fighting and cower into a defensive position. "No! Leave me alone!"

Wallis pulls a hand back to strike me into submission. And why not, I think defeatedly. The photo shoot's done. He doesn't need my face to be perfect anymore.

On that last bitter note, my skin feels a tingle of awareness before I hear, "What the fuck is going on out here? Are you okay?"

A savior. That's the first thought that crosses my mind. Someone's out here with us. My second is I don't know whether to feel humiliation or relief.

Wallis doesn't hesitate. He slaps his meaty paw across my mouth before answering, "She's fine."

A man steps into the shadows before declaring, "I'd like to hear the lady answer for herself."

Wallis snorts. "S'aint no lady. She's just a fuckin' . . ."

He doesn't get to disparage me any further. The stranger aims a kick into Wallis's gut before following him as he staggers away. The newcomer's voice washes over me like a balmy breeze as he growls, "Let me explain something."

As I scramble toward the light, the stranger takes his clasped hands and rams them under Wallis's chin. "Men don't treat ladies like this."

Wallis spits at the man's boots. "I tole you, s'ain't no lady. She's just a model."

My head drops in shame. God, how many people in the business have said something similar to me—from the time I began till now, when I'm at the height of my career.

"Wrong. Fuckin'. Answer." Wallis's head snaps back when the man gives him a right hook that has him spinning into the wall.

That's when my dark angel turns around and I get a good look at his face.

My throat closes when I recognize the mega country star. "You're . . . you're . . ."

Brendan Blake shrugs out of his jacket before draping it over my shoulders. "And you're you." He lifts my chin so his hazel eyes can peruse my face. His jaw clenches. "I'd ask if you're okay, Ms. Madison, but there's no way you can be."

My lips begin to tremble.

"That was pretty traumatic. It's okay to cry."

"I can't."

"You don't have to be strong."

I glance around him to Wallis crumpled against the wall before I whisper, "I won't cry until I get home."

"Ms. Madison, you don't have to be—"

"It's not the first time someone's tried . . . you know, with me," I interrupt. "I only wish I could say it was the first dozen. I need to go."

Brendan's lips tighten in anger. He spins on his heel so he's facing Wallis. "Excuse me while I go kill him."

"No, don't! Just let it go!"

Teeth barred, Brendan whirls around toward me. "Why shouldn't I tear this monster limb from limb?"

Hesitantly, I step forward and touch Brendan's arm. "Because on another night, another woman might need a complete stranger to rescue her. Don't let her down."

The tension clears from his face. He jerks up his chin. "How do you plan on getting out of here?"

In other words, *what's your plan to avoid the paparazzi downstairs?* We both know the place is crawling with them. I'm not certain which of us the papers mentioned more—country's up-and-coming star or me, the most famous face on the planet. The Incandesce launch party is being covered by at least a dozen papers and media outlets like MTV and ET. My publicist warned me that any news about this event should hit every major network by morning.

I twist my head to the side and stare out over the lights of Manhattan. "The same way I came in."

His head tilts to the side. "And how's that?"

My shoulders square beneath the warmth of his tuxedo jacket. "With my head held high, Mr. Blake. I did nothing wrong." Quickly, beneath the folds of his coat, I assess the damage to my borrowed, blush-colored Zac Posen original. I sigh in relief when I realize I can do a repair job that will easily hide beneath the matching cloak. "Fortunately, if I can borrow your jacket for just a few minutes and find my purse, I'll be able to do just that."

"Darlin', you can have anything of mine for as long as you need it," he replies. His eyes never leave my face.

I open my mouth to thank him again, but I can't formulate the words. Instead, I offer him a weak smile of gratitude before ducking back inside the party.

Ten minutes later, when I'm ready to make the great escape, I'm holding Brendan's jacket in my hand. Running my fingers over the fine wool, I murmur, "What the hell am I supposed to do with this?"

"Hand it over so I can put it on and escort you downstairs?" comes the whiskey-voiced suggestion from behind me.

I stiffen. "You were waiting for me?"

"Damn . . . darn straight I was. Those fu . . . ducking gossips were already startin' the second you came in off the balcony." His whiskey tone has a sharp dose of bitters spiked through it.

For some reason, his attempt to clean up his language causes my lips to twitch. Then the grief over what almost happened tonight washes over me again. "I apologize for causing you so much trouble, Mr. Blake."

He holds out his hand. I lay the jacket on it, feeling like I just lost a safety blanket. "Brendan."

I blink rapidly. "Excuse me?"

"Friends who let friends beat the sh . . . crud out of pieces of . . . turd should call each other by their first names. Right?" Without giving me a chance to respond, he shrugs on his jacket before holding out his arm gesturing for me to pass him.

We're in the elevator descending before I manage to mumble, "Friends and family call me Dani."

The flashbulbs pop the moment we alight from the elevator. Brendan rests his hand gently on my back, guiding me through the pack of vultures. I stiffen before I hear his voice rumble, "Hold tight, darlin'. I got you."

We finally get through the press and I'm seated in a waiting town car when I realize Brendan's not beside me. Disheartened, I realize I have no way of saying thank you—not for rescuing me. Not for helping me escape with my pride intact.

Nothing.

That's when I feel the first tear slide down my face because I know I'm alone again, wondering how to cope with this latest trauma.

A few moments later, my phone rings in my clutch. I flip it open and whisper, "Phina."

"I just arrived at the party, darling. We're supposed to be talking about your upcoming photoshoot. Where is your glorious face? Are you running late?"

"Just . . . forget about it."

There's silence on the other end. "Danielle? Are you all right?"

"I . . . have to go. I mean, thank you for the generous offer, but I . . . I won't be able to meet you."

The background noise of the party fades. "Danielle . . ."

"I'm . . . sorry. I . . ." My voice breaks.

"Wallis Hampton just walked in with a bloodied lip and is reaching for the booze," she proclaims.

I bite my lip so hard I can taste my own blood. Phina Hart and Wallis Hampton are contemporaries—both enormous names in the business.

"I sincerely pray whoever made him that way is sainted," she proclaims.

I can't quite choke back my sob.

"Tomorrow. You, me, all this is coming to an end."

I swallow the knot in my throat before whispering, "I don't know how."

"I do."

Phina disconnects right before the car pulls up in front of my brownstone. I slide from the car without a word to the driver and dash to the entrance to my haven of safety behind the doors protected by the night doorman.

CHAPTER THREE

Danielle

Fashionista41324: Danielle Madison was out with Phina Hart in New York City.

MarryMePhina02: What happened?

Danilleismygoddess17: (YAWN) No biggie. They're friends.

Fashionista41324: You're such a heathen, Goddess17. Do you want to know or not?

Danilleismygoddess17: Does it take me out
of the running for marrying Danielle
Madison?

MarryMePhina02: Ew. Gross.

Fashionista41324: No. But whatever she said
caused Phina to hurl one of Starbuck's
collector's mugs against the wall.

Danilleismygoddess17: Wait; you were
THERE?

Fashionista41324: Duh. They came into my
store.

**—Chat room dedicated to Danielle Madison
Sightings**

I scrub my fingers across my forehead as I desperately glance around to make certain Phina's antics don't garner us any unwanted attention. After shrieking at the top of her lungs, she drops next to me on the leather couch and wraps her thin arms around me. "Dani, god. I don't even know what to say."

"It's not like it's the first time a photographer groped one of us, Phina. You know this." My head tips to the side so it rests against hers. Phina, a model herself before she got behind the lens, knows the agony I suffer by my career choice. I make a rough sound. "I'm debating walking away. I'm not sure how much more I can handle before I break."

Her head snaps up and almost clocks me beneath the chin. "No, Danielle. They don't get to win."

Wearily, I gesture at the magazine laying on the coffee table in front of us. I'm on the cover, looking to everyone on seven continents as if I don't have a care in the world. "Who do you think they're going to believe, Phina? You and me? Get real."

The fashion industry as a whole has a layer of filth hidden beneath glossy covers and glitzy runways. Even though I was courted into the elite of modeling at eighteen, I've still been adamantly warned about who not to piss off, who to dress sexy for. And above all, when to keep my damn mouth shut.

After last night, I'm not certain that's a possibility anymore.

"Harassment is glossed over as excuses for measurements," Phina growls.

I mimic, "'Spread your legs just a little wider, sweetheart. That way, I can get the perfect fit.' God, if I had a dollar for every time that was accompanied by a hand 'accidentally' reaching too high."

"You and me both." She holds my hand, giving me a tight squeeze before saying, "What if I became your exclusive photographer?"

"Phina," I chide. "You can't do that."

She straightens her shoulders before bellowing, "I can do anything I damn well please!"

Even feeling as empty as I do, my lips can't help but curve at her antics.

Her mouth opens and closes. My brow quirks. "What is it?"

"I read you left the party with Honky Tonk last night. Was that just gossip or . . .?"

"He stopped Wallis. It's because of him that I . . ."

"Well, shit," she grumbles, annoyed.

I narrow my eyes at her. "What? Did you not want him to help me?"

She jams her shoulder into mine. "Don't be stupid."

"Then will you please explain?"

Phina mutters, "I hate I feel compelled to go out and listen to country music."

I scrunch my eyes closed and try to put her odd words together. Finally, I give up trying to translate Phina. "Nope. Still don't get it."

Instead of answering me, she snags her empty coffee cup from the table before hurling it at a wall. It splinters into chunks.

I suck in a breath at the immediacy of the attention cast toward our little bubble. "Well, if we didn't before, we definitely have everyone's attention now. Don't we?"

"Now is not the time to joke," she warns.

"I wasn't."

"Brendan. Blake. Saved. You!"

Still terrified by last night, I whisper, "Do you think I don't know that?"

Phina drops her voice to a whisper. "Do you think I don't hear the agony in your voice?"

"I know you do."

"I also know that despite his rising success, he's about to shoot off like a rocket."

"Why is everyone so certain of that?"

"Knowing this guy's signed with Wildcard? Due to drop his first studio album within the year? Get real."

That makes sense. Wildcard Music is the label to sign with. I'm on Small Town Night's latest album cover—one of their top acts. "I still don't get . . ."

"I'll buy a damned music store to support him. Do you hear me? There isn't anything I wouldn't do to thank him for stepping in to save you." Her voice takes on a faraway note. "I just wish there'd been a country boy who saved me before I became a shadow of myself."

Now it's my turn to comfort her. "You're not a shadow, Phina. You're a storm waiting to rain down hellfire."

She tunes back in to me. "Damn straight, which is why I'll be your exclusive photographer from now on unless we agree on the person?"

I sigh before acquiescing. "Talk to my agent. We'll draw up the contracts."

She snuggles close before whispering tragically, "How early do you think it starts?"

"What?"

"Their predatory behavior? Is it something they learn before they migrate to this city?"

I open my mouth to respond, but something niggles at the back of my brain. "Did you ever talk about this during sex ed?"

Phina shakes her head. "Just the mechanics in my generation. You?"

"No. It was a basic 'birds and bees' talk." I feel the churn of the same oily, greasy nausea from the night before when my mind twists in a direction it couldn't go toward in the dark. But now, in the light? "Phina, there are child models, actors. What if this is happening to them? What if they're not speaking up?"

Her jaw opens and shuts before she finally manages, "Dani, surely they would have told their parents, right?"

"Would they? I'm twenty-eight and I haven't told mine. Have you told yours?"

Her face pales. "No."

My heart beating in a rapid staccato, I look down at my shaking hands. "I need to think about this."

"About what?"

"About what we should do."

"Dani, who are we to do anything?"

I meet her dark gaze head-on before I remind her, "Seraphina, you and I are survivors."

She holds my eyes and murmurs, "Danielle Madison, you're a great deal more than that. I've never had a person in my life quite like you before."

"I hope that's a good thing."

"The best. Even if your face wasn't exquisite, I'd still want to take your picture because I know I'd see your heart through my lens."

Her words cause my lips to tremble. "I haven't done anything. I don't even know what it is we *should* do."

"Yet," she tacks on ruthlessly. She digs in her bag for her cell phone and flips it open to dial. Holding the phone to her ear, she barks, "Yes, this is Seraphina Hart. I need an appointment with Robert Watson, preferably this week."

I blink as she coolly informs the person on the other end, "Thursday will be excellent. No, I don't want to say what it's for. I'll inform him then." Without another word, she snaps the phone closed. "Let's get out of here. We have plans to make before we meet with my lawyer."

I pause her before she can spring into action. "Phina, why are we meeting with your lawyer?"

"Because—and you'll never hear me admit it in front of him—the man can get more done in two hours than I can in two months. It doesn't hurt he's absolutely gorgeous. Too bad he's married to his practice."

"Phina," I warn.

She regards me curiously. "What do you want to happen after last night?"

"I never want anyone to feel how I did. Ever again." She opens her mouth to speak, but I trample over her. "I know that's a pipe dream."

"You don't believe we can change the world?"

"You do?"

"Of course."

"How?"

"You're you, Danielle. You have the world at your feet. Use your power wisely."

I press a hand to my stomach, feeling the first stirrings of hope. "We can change how we feel."

"We will because you give strength to everyone effortlessly. You're the strongest woman I know."

"That's not true," I protest.

"You don't think so? In one night, you're already looking beyond your own pain. You could still be curled up and crying over a lot more than spilt milk, darling. And you don't believe you're indestructible? I'm grateful—regardless of our age difference—I found you to inspire my life."

"There has to be a future beyond pain," I whisper.

"We'll make it so." Phina's hand rubs my back. Abruptly, she stands. "Now, let me go bribe the young barista with a large tip to clean up my little tizzy and off we'll go to make plans."

"To make the world perfect?"

"As best as we can." With that, she strides away, leaving me with my thoughts.

Never have words made me feel quite so full of hope when I know down to the depths of my soul I'm lacking in faith, let alone courage. I know Phina wouldn't ever be anything but honest with me, but my soul clings to the frayed ends of my emotions out of sheer desperation.

It has to.

Otherwise how will I be able to cut away this ugly memory and move on?

CHAPTER FOUR

Brendan

As if it wasn't a given, Danielle Madison formally signed a contract to become the face of STORM. With an '80s flair to their merchandise branding, the model was overheard joking with friends, "Maybe I can donate buckets of money just to be asked to wear their clothes." It's no secret how much the supermodel has an affinity for all things from the '80s.

—**Models Weekly**

SPRING—TWENTY YEARS AGO

APPROACHING THE SET OF THE STORM PHOTOSHOOT, I'M PISSED as shit to be wasting precious time I could be spending with my family. Instead, I'm expected to be hamming it up for what? Some clothing line? "What a crock," I declare, flinging the outside door open wide.

The head of my record company—Kristoffer Wilde, the giant behind Wildcard Music—reminded me that with my first full-length album soon to be dropped, the goal is to reach out to a new audience, to people who aren't just hardcore country listeners. "Brendan, what you don't realize is you're as much of the package we're selling as your music."

I kept my mouth shut because Kristoffer gave me a chance when few would have. He heard me play "Broken Boots" in a seedy Nashville dive and hung around until after the show to talk. "I listened to your EP. It's impressive."

I almost swooned at the words. Kristoffer Wilde found my EP impressive. Me, Brendan Blake.

"I'd like to have a serious conversation with you about a full-length LP," Kristoffer said. His lip curled. "And about getting you out of dives like this."

"Dives like this are what pay the bills," I told him.

"Perhaps but not for much longer." That's when he handed me his card and informed me to be in his office in two days.

That night I went home and called my mom with the news, I honest to God thought she fainted over the phone. Wildcard Music signed me less than a month later. The first time I opened for Small Town Nights in Charleston a few months after Broken Boots got some serious airtime—I know for damn certain she did. I'm just grateful my road manager was there to catch her.

With a weary sigh, I run my hand through my hair as I shove the door open and am overpowered by Boston's "Piece of Mind" blaring out of the speakers. I mutter, "At least someone's got decent taste in music."

The rapid *click, click, click* of a camera tells me I'm either late or not the only celebrity who was roped into this campaign. The music has a short lull which gives me an opportunity to approach the director when I hear, "Awesome, Dani. Take a quick break before we pick it back up."

"Thanks, Phina!" is immediately returned in an enthusiastic tone by none other than Danielle Madison herself. Her smile is as blinding as the neon T-shirt she's wearing beneath a slim-fitting blazer.

Yet, her perkiness doesn't nothing but make me see red.

I storm past the photographer and onto the set where Danielle "my friends call me Dani" Madison is laughing with the individual unbuttoning the jacket she's wearing and ask, "What are you doing here?"

Her hair, done up in a bunch of messy blond curls, whips in my direction. Her purple eyes light with warmth before she holds out her hands. "Brendan. It's so good to see you again."

I back away.

Her expression transforms into one of confusion.

"Look, I don't need some supermodel's popularity to boost mine. I've got a pretty decent following of my own," I drawl laconically.

"I'm aware," she agrees, confused.

"Then why would you do something so asinine as to instigate a meetin' between us during a photo shoot I don't want to do?"

Silence descends on the set. A man wearing Day-Glo orange lipstick approaches Danielle cautiously. "Dani? Sugar? Is there a problem?"

"No, Jamal. It's my fault." She turns and flips him a bright smile.

"What is, sugar?"

"I misinterpreted Mr. Blake's desire to support STORM's mission based on our last encounter. It don't make no never mind." She reaches over and squeezes his arm. "Don't worry. I know for a fact Small Town Nights is coming in later. We'll just rearrange the story boards."

Jamal chews his lip before darting me a quick glance. Then he beams up at Danielle. "If you're sure."

She wraps her arm around his shoulders and leans down. "Darn straight I am." Danielle begins listing all of the celebrities involved with this project and I want to swallow my tongue. *Shit, whatever this is, is a massive deal.* She concludes with a cavalier, "We won't need Mr. Blake as one of our spokespeople."

My stomach begins to churn when I realize how much I jumped to the wrong conclusion. *What the hell is STORM?* I try to repair the damage. "Dani . . ."

The incensed look she shoots me could fry an egg. "That name is reserved for friends, Mr. Blake. Now, if you'll excuse us, we have some work to do, and this is a closed set."

I flinch at the acid lacing her tone. I can't say I blame her. I attacked her much in the same way that baboon did on the balcony did in New York, only I did it with words instead of with my hands.

I'm not certain which is worse.

Later that night after spending time with my family, I sit behind my desk and mentally thank God I insisted the builder put in hardwired jacks so I can connect to the Internet at high speeds instead of suffering the whoosh—whoosh of dial up. I pull up my e-mail and find a message from Kristoffer waiting.

From: Wilde, Kristoffer

To: Blake, Brendan

Subject: YOU ARROGANT, SNOT NOSED, PAIN IN MY ASS!

Do you know how many celebrities were gagging to be considered for the STORM project? No, of course not. And YOU were requested—specifically asked for. Why? Who the hell knows. Not that it matters now because it's not something that matters to BRENDAN BLAKE.

Christ, you haven't even put out your first album and here you are acting like a prima donna.

Let me reiterate, in case my subject line didn't give you an idea—I think you're self-centered, sanctimonious prick.

Do you even know what STORM's mission is? Again, of course not. You never asked me WHY I would send you on a photo shoot; you just bitched about it.

I have no idea why Danielle Madison thought YOU might give a damn about stopping sexual assault of children in the acting and modeling communities.

None.

THAT's what STORM is about.

Maybe it's time you stop being so caught up in yourself and think about someone else.

I sure as hell hope you give a damn about something, someone, Brendan. I'd hate to see your star burn out the way so many other's have because they don't find it within themselves to care.

—KW

"I think I'd have preferred a bomb explode," I grate out.

"What was that, B?" A sweet voice—with an accent that's a mixture of upper-crust British and formal American—pipes up from my office doorway.

My head whips away from the reaming I rightfully deserved, and I struggle to keep my composure when shiny dark hair bounces as the bombshell in the making makes her way around the desk to stand next to me.

She points at the screen. "It doesn't sound like you're being a terribly good role model, Brendan."

I run my hand over her silky hair—hair we inherited from our jackass of a father. "I screwed up."

Our father's eyes narrow when she glances over her shoulder at me. That's when Ursula prompts, "Then promise me you'll make it right."

"I promise, princess."

She clutches my arm in a grip a wrestler couldn't break before hesitantly pressing a kiss to my cheek—something that makes me want to bury my father. Unfortunately, with the loss of Ursula's mother so fresh in her mind, I can't go after the old man for the abominable way he's treating his youngest child. All I can do is be here for these precious moments we're granted together. She yawns, lifting a delicate hand to her mouth. "Tomorrow, can we practice driving again?"

I tug at her ear. "Not a chance while we're here in the city."

She pouts. "I'm turning sixteen soon. I'm supposed to be getting in as much practice as possible."

"Which we'll do when we get back to Tennessee."

"Fine." The word is drawn out to be at least three syllables.

"You just want to drive better than Joshua when you return to England," I accuse. Our other brother—a mere eight months older than Ursula—is irritated she's visiting me already while our father sent him to Birmingham for soccer camp. *Shit, football,* I mentally correct myself as Ursula's done umpteen times. Just today he called and declared, "He can sod off, B. I want to be *home* with both of you!"

The fact I've managed to keep both of my half-siblings concealed from the paparazzi that follows up my ass is a minor miracle. That they consider either of my houses more of a home than they one share with our father, uber billionaire West Moore, elates, terrifies, and infuriates me.

Sula's lips curve in a smile I know is going to give me sleepless nights when she really focuses on boys and starts dating. "Well, duh."

I can't help but laugh outright. "We'll get your practice in, I promise, but not in the city. There isn't a chance in hell I'm letting you burn out my clutch."

She rolls her eyes in exasperation before giving in to the good sense she taught herself since she inherited it from neither of her parents. Before she gets a foot away from me, she aims her emerald green eyes my way. My stomach roils. One day, I'm going to have to kill a man for being on the receiving end of this look, I just know it. Then she growls, "Fix whatever you did."

"Sweet dreams, Sula. Shut the door behind you."

"'Kay. Night, B."

After Sula's long gone, I pull up STORM's website. That's when I find out Danielle Madison and a few members of the fashion industry—including celebrity photographer Phina Hart—transformed Danielle's negative experience the night we met into a call-to-action. A New York Times article I linked to from the site reads, "Unilaterally approved by the governments of the states of New York and California for funding to educate teachers and administrators about how to handle children who come forward when they've been in harmful situations, Danielle Madison and Phina Hart's mission is evolving into a nationwide initiative. Now, both women are considered ambassadors for this cause.

"When asked what drove her passion for this project, she admitted it was the person who saved her from a similar fate at a party in New York City. 'He has no idea how he changed the course of my life by storming into an unknown situation instead of standing silent on the sideline.'"

With that, I rise and hurl my chair into the wall before moving over to the bank of windows that overlooks the city. I stare at my reflection in absolute disgust. The man whose image is reflected back at me appears weary and exhausted. I ask aloud, "Why did you get so pissed at her?"

Because she caused you to break away from the image you were cultivating to piss off your father. And if you hadn't? What would have happened to Danielle Madison then?

I don't bother replying to my inner thoughts. Instead, I ask my image, "How long do you think you can keep your secrets hidden? Do you really think you can be who you want to be and protect the kids at the same time?"

When I can't find an easy answer, I reach over and snag the cordless phone to arrange for my mother and Smith to stay with Sula tomorrow so I can head back to Fort Washington to grovel. After the phone clatters back into the charger, I start rehearsing my apology. Unable to find something appropriate for the level of jackass I displayed, I mutter, "Christ, it will serve me right if she doesn't forgive me."

For long moments, I stand there wondering if I have a chance at making this right or if I'm perfectly insane to try.

CHAPTER FIVE

Danielle

Charitable donations for storm skyrocketed as the tear sheets of celebrities impacted by sexual assault in the workplace were released to the media.

Fashion photographer Phina Hart, supermodel Danielle Madison, and country music star Amanda Reidel from Small Town Nights were just a few of those featured.

—Mode Entertainment

The Next Day

I'm standing alone at the warehouse where we've been shooting the last few days in Fort Washington. Here and there, people are arriving for what we know will be another hectic day.

Distracted from my confrontation with Brendan, I'm drawn to the schedule boards for the shoot. My hair is in pigtails which sway back and forth as my lips form a moue of disgust when I see his name crossed out with a thick black line. I whisper, "Damn you, Brendan."

"I'd damn me to hell and back too," comes a quiet voice from beside me.

I still, but my hair doesn't. I wind up with the curls smacking me across my eyes and nose. I scrunch up my nose even as I verbalize my irritation. "Ouch."

Brendan chuckles softly at my hair's usual antics. "I take it that's not the first time that's happened?"

"Nor will it be the last." Once I swipe my hair off my face, I find his lined with regret. Belligerently, I demand, "Why are you here?"

His eyes drift to the schedule. "To see if I can erase the black mark against me."

"Proverbially?"

"Literally. Danielle, I owe you—everyone here, actually—an enormous apology. I had no idea why I was sent here, but that's really no excuse for the way I behaved."

"No, it isn't."

Brendan's head dips in shame.

"Everyone on this set is a victim. More importantly, they're survivors. Sometimes, that's because they had someone like the *you* I met the night of the party come into their lives," I hiss fiercely.

His head lifts. Our eyes connect and just that quickly, my heart tumbles over and over in my chest like a bouncing ball. Quickly I tell myself, *Wrong place. Wrong guy.*

Then he reminds me why it may be the wrong place, but he might be the right guy after all. "As of late, too many people make demands on the man they want me to be. Sometimes I forget the man I was brought up as."

"And who is that?" I challenge him.

"Human."

I think about the meaning behind his words before I acknowledge his sentiment. "I can appreciate that."

"I thought you might." He reaches up and brushes one of my pigtails. "This is a good look for you."

"Childlike?" I offer the adjective most used by my family when they see this particular hairstyle.

His head shakes back and forth. "Happy."

I press my lips together and twist my head away. *This is the man I was hoping would show up yesterday.* Then I spy Phina over by the coffee service. Making a split-second decision, I grab Brendan's hand. "Come with me."

He doesn't object but asks, "Where?"

"Just trust me."

Half an hour later, Phina calls out to Brendan over the sound of ZZ Top. "You know, Honky Tonk, you're killing my schedule. What do I get for it?"

He winks at her before aiming a wicked smile at the camera. The STORM T-shirt molded to his chest makes parts of me quiver in excitement. To cover my reaction, I bounce up and down like a cheerleader. Brendan smirks in response to my antics before drawling laconically, "Please tell me there's photos somewhere of Danielle doing just that."

Phina snickers behind the lens. "She's always bouncing around. If she's not in heels, it's aerobics for the insane at any of her shoots."

"Hey!" I stick my tongue out at my friend.

"Don't even try to deny it, missy," is tossed drolly in my direction as Phina keeps shooting at Brendan with rapid-fire clicks.

I sniff. "I wasn't going to. I was simply going to remind you, I'm like this in heels too."

Brendan bursts into laughter. His face noticeably softens when our eyes clash and hold.

Phina lowers her camera, her long nail tapping the lens case. "Dancing Queen, stop your shenanigans behind me. Get yourself up there next to Honky Tonk."

I bounce-skip next to Phina, demanding in a loud whisper, "What are you doing?"

"I see a lot behind the lens, darling. Sometimes, I like seeing things in front of it."

"Phina," I warn.

She fiddles with her settings murmuring, "Go stand next to your storm chaser and let me take a few pictures."

Brendan quirks a brow when I trudge my way onto the set. "Don't look so pleased, Dancing Queen."

I burst out laughing before socking him in the arm.

He grips my fist and lifts it to his mouth in a very courtly gesture. Charmed, despite myself, I curtsey. Someone jacks up the music and the next thing I know, Brendan's twirling me under his arm.

I step back before I do a heel out, heel together. Twist, jump, clap. Shimmy. Shake. My pigtails are jiggling and I'm laughing like a loon.

Brendan just smiles at me indulgently before snagging my hand again and we repeat the pattern over and over until we reach the song's crescendo. He takes both of my hands and twists them over my head. We spin round and round until we end up pressed against one another, breathless.

Without giving it much thought, I lean up and press my lips against his cheek. "Thank you for chasing the storm away."

Before I can dash off to greet the next in a long line of celebrities due to have their photos taken, he lightly clasps me around the waist. "If I promise to take more care with you, would you have dinner with me tonight?"

"I don't need you to be careful, Brendan."

"You're saying no?" Disappointment rings in every syllable.

I set my curls to dancing and I can't help but grin when they whack him on the side of his face. Instead of being irritated, he smiles down at me. He bites his lip, pulling the full lower one up between his white teeth, forcing my eyes to it. In my chest, my heart starts a rapid staccato I can barely control. "I'm saying yes. Don't make me regret trusting you."

"You won't. I swear." He braces his hands on his hips, giving me a cocky smirk. "Where should I pick you up?"

"Right here. I've got many more people to harangue into doing my bidding." I toss him a sassy look filled with a confidence I'm faking for all I'm worth as I leave him in the middle of the set, deliberately bumping Phina's shoulder as I pass by her.

His laughter rings through my mind for the rest of the day.

CHAPTER SIX

Brendan

Brendan Blake flew to New York City as part of the STORM campaign. "People close to me have experienced sexual assault. I fully support them and the mission of STORM."

One wonders if his support is partly due to co-founder Danielle Madison. It wasn't that long ago the two were spotted leaving the *Incandesce* party together.

When Wildcard Music was questioned if there's any truth to the rumors swirling about the duo, they declined to comment.

—New York Entertainment

The warehouse is still brightly lit when I pull back up at five o'clock. There are a few cars and vans peppered around the lot, but for the most part it's empty. I grow uneasy when I think of Danielle waiting here alone for me to pick her up. I throw my car in park, shove my door open, and stride into the STORM studio space.

I slow my approach when I do because Danielle isn't alone.

"I do know how to do my own makeup, Phina."

Phina steps back and eyes her critically. "For the camera, yes. For a date? You'd sooner slap on your John Deere hat and your cousin's jeans and call it a day."

Much to my amusement, Danielle's cheeks flush bright red. "There are days I hate you know me so well."

Proving she has a third eye in the back of her head, Phina calls out, "What do you think, Honky Tonk? Does she look presentable for wherever you're taking her?"

"More than. Though I have to admit, I wouldn't have minded seeing her in the John Deere hat," I drawl.

At Danielle's hopeful expression, a beatific smile passes over Phina's face. "Not on the first date, darling."

My laughter rings out over Danielle's groan of agony. "Thanks, Phina. Remind me to return the favor with your man of the week."

The man I recognize as Jamal comes out and slips his arm around Phina. "No need, Dani. I've already seen the worst of both of you."

I cough loudly. "Hey, new guy here. I wouldn't mind seeing some photos."

Phina says in a *sotto* voice. "Oh, I'm certain you would be eternally entertained."

Danielle stands and makes her way to me, hands extended. "Hi, Brendan. I'm so glad we made your third visit to the warehouse just as interesting as the first two."

I clasp hands in mine and pull her in closer so I can absorb the impact of the delicate floral scent on her skin. As remarkable as her hair and makeup are, I admit, "I kind of miss the pigtails."

A smile unlike those I've seen on the million magazine covers she's graced crosses her face. "Compliments like that earn you the best dinner of your life."

I release her hands before hooking my thumbs in the pockets of my dress jeans. "Know where I might be able to get a date for a meal like that at the last minute?"

Her lips quirk. "Maybe. Do you like seafood?"

"I'm a country boy from just outside of Nashville."

"Does that mean you have an aversion to fish?"

"Only the kind that still has its eyeballs when it's served."

She doesn't respond to my quip. Instead, she loops an arm through mine. "Bye, Phina."

"I'll try not to be too jealous," Phina calls back as she curls into the man still sporting the Day-Glo lipstick.

Even in heels, I still have an inch or so on Danielle, but our eyes are level. "I assume she's not jealous about the date."

"No, just my thought about dinner."

"I take it you have somewhere specific you'd like to go?"

"All depends on you."

We exit the building, and a black town car pulls up. The driver exits the vehicle and opens the back door. "What does?"

"Scale of one to ten, how hungry are you?" Her eyes gleam with anticipation.

"Hmm, between a two and three. Just starting to work up an appetite."

"How about I take you to the best seafood restaurant I know. It's a bit of a trek to get there, but worth the travel."

"What constitutes a trek?" I ask as I hand her into the back of the car before sliding in beside her.

Danielle crosses her legs to give me room. The move also almost causes my heart to fail as it pulls the material of her jeans even tighter. "About eighty minutes."

I may not be a dyed-in-the-wool New Yorker, but, "Even I know that's not horrendous."

That's when she shocks me. "By air." While I'm gaping at her, she leans forward and orders the driver to take us to Teterboro Airport. She sits back before announcing, "I want to spend time with you tonight, Brendan. Not you, me, and half of the paparazzi in New York City."

I don't just like this idea, I love it. When I tell her that, she gives me the same smile I received in the warehouse. Something near my heart squeezes. I realize I could quickly become addicted to it, to her.

I can't allow that to happen.

After all, I know better than anyone what happens when someone gets too close to your heart.

CHAPTER SEVEN

Danielle

Celebrating its 26ᵗʰ anniversary on Nantucket's harbor, Straight Wharf boasts one of the most choice views on the island of Nantucket.

Truly, though, is there a bad one?

—Tourist Trap

An SUV is parked on the tarmac waiting for me when we touch down in Nantucket about ninety minutes later. Brendan wraps his arm around my shoulder as we climb out of the helicopter and duck beneath the blades. As we're about to clear them, his mouth presses next to my ear and he shouts, "How will we get back?"

I twist my head and my lips brush the shell of his. "They'll wait."

He nods before coming to a screeching halt at the sight of a blond-haired man rounding the hood. Instinctively, I catch the keys pitched at me underhanded with one hand. Fortunately, the roar of the blades has slowed so I can shout, "Is that any way to greet me? We haven't seen each other in what?"

"Three glorious months."

"You are an ass, Jake," I inform him sweetly.

"And you're a rotten influence. How much more can you try to spoil my child?"

I stomp my foot. "She deserves it."

"Dani, I can send her to college if I sell off her wardrobe. Christ, what does a fifteen-year-old need with a Zac Posen original."

Haughtily, I inform him, "Like you said, it's an investment."

He scrubs his hand over his face before holding it out to Brendan. "Jake Madison. Dani's my cousin."

Brendan grips his hand firmly. "Brendan. Great to meet you. Do you live on the island?"

Jake grins. "Nah, we're all just crashing at her place."

Brendan's arm tightens around me. "You own a place on Nantucket?"

"Remember I mentioned I could relax here?" At his nod, I continue, "Ever since we were little—"

"Like eight or nine," Jake interjects.

"We've always come here for family vacations. It made sense to buy a place for the family."

Brendan's face pales. "Are we having dinner with your family?"

"Good God, no!"

Brendan's shoulders begin to shake. "You had me scared there for a minute, Dancing Queen."

"Brendan's met Phina, I see," Jake remarks drolly. He leans over and presses a kiss to my cheek. "Go. Have fun. And I won't spill the beans you're here."

I step away from Brendan and stare at the haggard face of my cousin before I hug him tightly. When I pull back, I tell him, "It will get better."

"Will it?" Jake pulls back and flicks his hand at us before heading toward the terminal entrance.

I stare after him for a moment before turning to Brendan. "Sorry. Family stuff."

"You're close?"

I gesture he should make his way to the car. He slides into the passenger seat without protest. After I get behind the wheel, I agree. "We are. Our fathers are twins. Jake and I were raised more like siblings than cousins. In fact, we grew up next door to one another."

There's a very visible struggle on his face as he absorbs my words. While he figures out what he wants to say next, I slip the key into the ignition and start the engine before heading toward downtown Nantucket. Finally, he says something I'll never forget because it might be the moment I began to fall a little in love with him. "You'll never know how fortunate you are to have such a close relationship with your family, Danielle. That's worth more than anything money could buy."

I take my eyes off the road long enough to give him a quick smile. "Trust me, I'm well aware of that. What's your family like?"

Brendan begins to tell me about his mother and how she's dating his tour manager, Smith. As I downshift, I jab him in the side. "So, what you're really saying is you have to be an angel when you're out on tour because otherwise, your mama's going to find out about it?"

One second. Two seconds. Then, Brendan groans. "Shit. I didn't even think of that."

My smile is wide and carefree as I cruise past the cranberry fields before aiming towards town. "Family is always where you least expect them."

"You have no idea how true that is." Then his stomach rumbles. "Oops."

I laugh. "Hungrier than you thought?"

"You have no idea." The huskiness in his words sends that ever-present tingle that ignites when he's near shimmering down my spine.

"I think you'll enjoy—"

Brendan lays his hand on top of mine on the gear shift and my mind blanks. All thought eludes me.

"Danielle?"

"I . . . it's . . . remember . . . Dani . . . friends," I somehow manage to stutter.

His fingers tighten over mine. "I'll stick with Danielle. I like being a little different to you."

Yeah, the cliff my heart's managed to avoid going over is looming in front of me just like it did for Thelma and Louise. To cover my worry, I begin chattering about the kind of delights Straight Wharf has on the menu.

"You were right."

I'm munching on a bite of my haricots verts. When I finish chewing, I query, "About?"

"About it being the best seafood I've ever eaten. Do the owners have any plans to open a restaurant in Nashville?" His face is so hopeful, I hate to dash his dreams.

"Not a chance. They shut down Columbus Day weekend and won't reopen until the spring."

He frowns down at his plate of swordfish. "Well, damn."

"I know." My eyes scan the busy restaurant in the distance. At my request, a private table was set up far away from the other patrons. "Even though my parents still live in the house I grew up in, I feel able to breathe here. Maybe that's because I've come here every time life's fallen to pieces."

Brendan's fork clatters to his plate. My lips twist wryly. "Too much information?"

"Not enough. What do you mean, fallen to pieces?"

I start to wave it off, but the intensity of his gaze draws me in. "I'm in my late twenties, Honky Tonk. I was eighteen when I started modeling. That's a lot of years to put up with a lot of crap."

"You mean like what happened in the city."

"It's almost ritualistic. You know you're a success the more you're . . . handled."

"Does your family know?" Before I can answer, he growls, "I only met him for half a minute, but I can't imagine your cousin letting you put up with that kind of crap, Danielle."

"My mom does. I was living a life they still don't fully understand. Back then? They would have been devastated. Now, I can explain what happened and make my mother appreciate I lived through it."

"I bet she's still ravaged by it."

My lips curve sadly. "You don't have a large family, right?"

He hesitates slightly before responding, "Right."

"Then your intuition is remarkable. Yes, she was, is," I correct myself. But I need to get my point across to the man sitting across from me, struggling with a decision I made long before he swooped into my life. "Brendan, the decision to not speak then, even the one to speak now, wasn't one I made lightly."

Needing to lighten the mood, I change the subject. "Be sure to save room for dessert. They make a lemon and blueberry pie here that's to die for.

In fact"—I twist around trying to find our waiter—"I might order a whole one to bring back to New York."

Brendan stares at me a moment before lifting his own fork and sawing off a bite of swordfish. "You're an enigma, Danielle."

"I'm just a woman," I protest.

"You are so much more than that." At the searing look he flings at me, I'm certain my scallops must now be overcooked and my skin is ten degrees warmer than it was ten seconds ago. "So, tell me about this pie. I haven't met one yet I don't like."

At that, I inform him haughtily, "If I could bathe in it, I would."

Brendan roars with laughter just as our waiter approaches. He pauses discretely at our table. "Is there something you need, Ms. Madison?"

It's Brendan who answers for us, still chortling. "Apparently, we need large slices of pie."

I just smile, anticipating his reaction when he tastes it.

CHAPTER EIGHT

Brendan

Did you think the Battle of Fort Washington was over? According to two recent investors in the area, it's just beginning. Renovations to the warehouse sold by the Corcoran Group in Fort Washington have been completed.

The new owners, who remain anonymous, are ready to open their doors to what's anticipated to be the city's next hottest nightclub.

Prior to its completion, part of the space was loaned to supermodel Danielle Madison and celebrity

photographer Phina Hart to shoot the STORM campaign.

Locals are eager for the official unveiling. However, rumors of formal invitations stating "*all who attend must seek redemption*" are popping up around the city.

—New York Entertainment

Long after I fought Danielle for the last bite, I'm still thinking about the way the flaky crust melted on my tongue. "I should have got one to go too."

Danielle pats the box sitting beside her in the seat with the hand I'm not holding triumphantly. "Told you so."

"So you keep saying."

Even though the pilot can undoubtedly hear us, Danielle ignores him and informs me, "I love night flying."

I squeeze her fingers. "Do you?"

"Floating in the air at night is a chance to let all your worries drift away before you wake up and have to battle them again tomorrow." Her profile, lit by the full moon, turns contemplative. "Maybe that's why we dream."

"I thought it was because it was piecing together parts of your memory," I say, recalling something I read when trying to help Joshua with one of his research papers long distance.

"I've never heard that, but aren't we saying the same thing? A mind can only travel so far before it needs a rest. Dreams happen all the time. I just prefer to be awake for mine." Her face turns toward me.

It would be easy to dismiss this exquisite woman as nothing more than a face. Maybe it was the circumstances under which we met, but some miracle is being bestowed upon me to allow me to delve beneath the fine bone structure the world is entranced by. "Right now, so do I."

I lift her fingers to my lips and brush my mouth across the knuckles. Through the cans we're wearing, I hear her breath catch. Then I gently shatter the spell weaving between us by saying, "I'm headed back to Nashville tomorrow."

"Oh. So soon?" The disappointment in her voice sends a surge of elation through me.

"I have a few things to see to at my place there," I reply simply. Like Joshua's arrival. Plus, if I don't get Sula out of this city, she's likely to steal my car, I think wryly.

I can feel her inquisitiveness even through the darkness. There's silence between us for a few minutes before she offers, "Then thank you for today and tonight, Brendan."

It's an out. I know she's giving it to me with no strings, no recriminations. I should take it and run—return to the life I'm destined to live in solitude, but I can't force my fingers to let hers go. Instead, I blurt, "When we land, I'll give you my number. This way we can talk until I return to New York in a few weeks."

"You don't have to—"

"I know," I interrupt. "I want to."

"Good?" Her voice squeaks as she turns her acquiescence into a question.

Amused, I lean toward her and nuzzle her cheek before placing a chaste kiss against it. This close, I see a hint of anxiety as she bites her lower lip. "How is it possible you're nervous around me, Dancing Queen? After all we've been through today?"

To my surprise, she blurts out, "Because I'm afraid of messing whatever this is up."

"You're afraid?" I repeat carefully.

"You're different, Brendan. I like different."

I'm saved from responding as the skids touch down. Danielle reaches up and removes her cans. I jerk mine off. Her voice lacks the radio transmission's tinny quality when she announces, "We're back."

I look around and my eyes bulge when I realize we're not at Teterboro. We're in the parking lot of the warehouse in Fort Washington. "How did you manage this?"

She shrugs one shoulder. "The owners of the building work at a club downtown. Decent guys. They don't mind me using the space as a heliport for now while they do renovations. The part we were in today is the last to be updated."

Before I can ask her what it's to become, the door next to her opens and the pilot helps Danielle from the chopper. She snatches the pie up before she leaps down. I swiftly follow her, instinctively ducking beneath the blades still spinning overhead. Danielle shakes the pilot's hand before the man sprints around and slides back into the cockpit.

We stand together as the little bird lifts off. Two cars are waiting to take us in two different directions a few hundred yards away. Yet, I can't help saying, "You'll call?"

Her smile turns wonky when she says, "I don't have anything to write down your number."

I slip my hand inside my jacket pocket and pull out the pen I lifted from our waiter after I signed the dinner check. Tugging the pie away from her, I scribble my private line across the top of the pastry box. "Now you do."

Her eyes flicker from the box top to me. "You really want me to call?"

In her expression, I find wariness and hope mixed with a healthy dose of interest. I slide my hand through the back of her hair, clasping her neck before pulling her face toward mine. Our lips are on an even level, our breaths jagged. "I want to kiss you."

"Then why aren't you?"

"Because I need to appreciate what you've given me today, tonight. I want you to understand that despite our very auspicious beginning, I was raised right by a mama who would horsewhip me for taking advantage after what I put you through in the last twenty-four hours. That means our first kiss is not happening in an abandoned parking lot."

"But it means there will be one."

I lean forward, mere millimeters separate her lips from mine. "Count on it."

This close, I can see the purple of her irises eclipsed almost entirely by her pupils. I murmur, "I'll walk you to your car." I slide an arm around her waist, and we begin the trek to our vehicles together.

Still clutching the pie box, she says, "Either you really want me to call, or you're trying to woo me into turning over my pie."

"I really want you to call." This time, the overhead lights give me the gift of being able to see her luminous smile. "That being said, you can keep the box, but can I have the pie?"

"I look forward to talking with you, but not that much," she informs me sweetly.

My whole body shakes with my laughter. Soon, so does hers.

CHAPTER NINE

Brendan

A child needs your love the most when he deserves it the least.

—Erma Bombeck

"We agreed," Sula begins hotly.

"We agreed to driving lessons. Not to you and Joshua taking my truck and doin' donuts in the backyard without my permission," I bite out harshly.

Joshua's lower lip trembles and tears well up in my sister's eyes at my righteous anger. It's Joshua who bravely asks, "Do . . . do you want us to leave?"

Sula makes a desperate grab for his hand. "Please, don't send us back to him, B. We'll fix things."

"And how do you propose you do that, Ursula?" I drawl laconically.

"I—we—will figure something out. Please don't send us back to West."

Shoving a hand through my hair in frustration, I shout, "I'm not sending you back to him when I just went through hell to get you here." Both of them visibly shudder in relief. "However I'm still royally pissed off. You're both grounded."

They beam at me as if I'd just handed them a mall gift card instead of doling out a punishment.

I study their faces and find myself wondering how the old bastard could sire three children and not one looks like him. Sula and I have the same hair color and my mother claims Joshua and I have the same lips and chin. None of us bear a striking resemblance to each other except for Joshua and Sula's eye color—a clear emerald, jewelers would salivate over if they found a stone that matched the intensity.

When I asked my mother why she stayed with West as long as she had when I found out Joshua was going to be born, she answered, "I thought he could give you things I couldn't, Brendan. Then, one day, I realized you weren't growing up to be a smart, intelligent child because of your father but in spite of him. That's what convinced me to file for divorce."

Now, staring at my siblings, I better understand why my mother made those early life decisions she made. Though they're his, the reality is Sula and Joshua are mine. And there's nothing I wouldn't do to protect them.

Even lie to the world.

The phone on my nightstand rings as my fingers pluck out a new melody on my favorite acoustic guitar. I'm in bed, back against the headboard. Snippets of the last few days flash through my mind, and my fingers tell the story of every moment between myself and Danielle Madison.

My fingers dance as I recall bounces, flashes, a queen to my king. All that Danielle Madison promises to be mixed in with the goof I already know she is.

I mark where I am on the notepad beside me before answering with a husky, "Hello?"

"Hello, is Brendan there, please?" Her request is so sweet. So polite. So full of shit since we exchanged all phone and email information during our first call three nights ago, and I explicitly told her I was the only person to answer this line.

And she also let slip during one of the moments just before she fell asleep with the phone tucked up to her ear, she "is monumentally disappointed your lips didn't taste mine before we parted ways, Brendan. I feel like I was robbed."

"Well, aren't we polite in our phone greetings, Danielle."

Her voice teases. "You could have acquired staff in the last twenty-four hours, Brendan. It's been known to happen."

I snort. "Nope. I still clean my own toilets, Danielle. Well, that is if my mother doesn't beat me to it."

"Oh my god. You too? My mother scrubs my place from floor to ceiling every time she visits. Nothing is sacred."

"I thought it was just me. I was afraid I was going to have to have a talk with her. I'm a grown man."

I can practically visualize her pigtails slapping her face as she swooshes her head back and forth. "Won't help. Mom still shows up with a bucket, pail, and Mr. Clean every month."

"Mine likes Pine-Sol."

"It's no secret I prefer lemon. If Mom's going to clean my place, she knows she'd better use the right stuff."

"Like I could forget your love of lemon. Or blueberry."

"Best combination in the world," she mumbles.

Uh-huh. Casually, I ask, "Speaking of, is there any pie left?"

"Umm . . ."

My voice growls, "Danielle?"

"Well, I'm kind of eating it right now."

"You're having another slice while you're on the phone with me?"

"Not a slice, per se."

"A bite?" I'm hoping that when I head back to New York next week, there might be some leftover, even if it's just a nibble. Enough that I might be able to taste it on her lips when I kiss her for the first time.

"More like I slapped the pie pan onto a plate and brought a fork," she admits.

"I can't even be jealous because that's . . ."

"What?"

"Exactly something I'd do." We both crack up.

We trade quips back and forth for a while before she yawns. "I hate to end our conversation early tonight, but Phina's shooting me by the Hudson for a new perfume advertisement at sunrise."

"Then sleep well, Dancing Queen."

"Night, Honky Tonk."

She hangs up the phone and I pick up my guitar and begin strumming again, smiling as I think about all the things I'm learning about Danielle Madison that fit brilliantly in my life.

If only I'd allow someone to be a permanent part of it.

The next morning, there's a ring at the door. Sula jumps up from her chair. "I'll get it."

Standing at the stove scrambling eggs for the three of us, I call out, "Thanks, kid."

A few moments later, she comes back juggling a flat box. "B, the delivery guy said it has to remain this side up."

I frown even as I stare at the box labeled "Perishable" on all sides. "Okay."

Sliding the eggs off the burner, I gesture to breakfast before slipping my hand into my pocket for the utility knife I snagged off the dresser this morning. "Did it come with a card?"

"Not that he handed to me." Sula wrinkles her nose at the slightly over-cooked toast before taking a scoopful of eggs and more than her ration of bacon. Joshua doesn't hesitate on any of it before almost wiping out the rest of the food.

But as I stare at the contents of the box, I realize that's okay. I know what I'll be eating for breakfast.

Lunch.

Dinner.

Absolutely for dessert.

Joshua, a mouthful of eggs and using his fork to point at the box, asks, "What's in there?"

I lift the perfectly baked blueberry-lemon pie that somehow made it from Nantucket to Nashville before informing them, "Something incredible."

Sent by a woman that could be absolutely perfect for me if life didn't have different plans.

And they don't involve a ridiculously beautiful supermodel who would track down my address to send me a pie.

CHAPTER TEN

Brendan

Freud wrote that "dreams are often most profound when they are the most crazy."

Does this long-held belief play into why the decriminalization of marijuana is being hotly debated?

If we act now, it could add billions to our economy, create hundreds of thousands of jobs, free up police resources, and stop racial disparities in marijuana enforcement that tie up our court systems.

—Anonymous Letter to the Collyer Courier Editor

She's ethereal in a floor length white gown, long blond curls falling free but pulled away from her face.

Even though her expression is cool, remote, she knows I'm there. I know it especially with the way her eyes flick to the side when she passes where I'm sitting.

To the rest of the world, I'm not there. I could be anyone, anything.

She'll pay for that little move later, I think to myself. I'm aroused and amused as she passes by rather than frustrated. Yet, as always, I'm flabbergasted when the sheer perfection of her face is lit up by the spotlight. Her expression doesn't change, though her gown does as each crystal takes life.

As beautiful as the dress is, it doesn't hold a candle to the woman wearing it.

I'm almost brought to my knees when her perfect body turns. As she strides around the catwalk, I have a clear view over the patrons' heads. The ripeness of her stomach steals my breath away.

My fingers tighten around the neck of the guitar I'm holding, the frets imprinting grooves against my calloused fingers. I brought it to her as an offering. Hell, I'd offer her my life if I believed that was what this elusive woman needed in order to love me.

Just before she slips off the stage, I'm staggered when her head whips in my direction. For all her aloofness in front of the world, she becomes mine with a single look—a look that burns away all pretenses of who and what she was made to love.

My brow furrows even as my eyes snap open. My covers are down around my feet as I shoved them off when I attempted to race after my dream woman with my guitar in hand. With a sigh, I realize both my chase and sleep are futile at this point. Scrubbing my hands over my face, I mutter, "She's following me into my dreams. This can't be a good sign."

No, but I can't stay away from her.

Danielle Madison isn't a woman I'll ever be able to forget.

Not now, possibly not ever.

Even if she walks away.

CHAPTER ELEVEN

Danielle

"People ask me what I do in winter when there's no baseball. I'll tell you what I do. I stare out the window and wait for spring."

—Rogers Hornsby

"What are you wearing for your date with Honky Tonk?" Phina asks.

I have her on speaker as I'm braiding my hair so I can shove on a baseball cap. "I don't even know where we're going. All he said was to be ready by one."

"It doesn't sound like it's going to be too fancy."

"That's what I was going with."

There's a pause before an enormous groan. "Please, Danielle, do not wear that atrocious hat."

I glare at the phone though it has no impact on Phina. "Don't start, Phee. You know my dad works for John Deere. I love this hat."

"What if he's taking you to Tavern On the Green?"

I snort. "Not likely."

"He might surprise you."

I reach for the hat in question, tugging it over my head. "Unlikely."

"What else are you wearing?"

I'm about to answer Phina when the doorbell rings. "Got to go."

Phina shouts, "Have fun!" just as I press the button to disconnect the call.

I snatch up the phone and slip it into the pocket of my Bermuda shorts. Once I reach the front door and ascertain it's Brendan, all my worries disappear when I get a load of his outfit. I quickly undo the locks and fling the door open wide. "Sneakers? You own them?"

He runs his eyes down my legs to find my feet similarly attired. "It's obviously not a crime."

"Come on inside. I just need to grab my purse."

He steps up to me and drags his fingers down my cheek. "I didn't realize how much I missed seeing you until just now."

My heart begins to race at the simple words and the profound meaning behind them. "Me too. I mean, I missed seeing you as well. Not me, I see me every day."

Brendan grins, and all thoughts fly from my head. I mumble, "I just need a minute."

He glances down at his watch. "We have a few before we have to worry about being late."

Once he crosses the threshold, I give in to the need to brace myself against the front door. The rear view of Brendan Blake in shorts and a T-shirt is as impressive as the front. That's when I notice what's tucked in his back pocket. Regaining my equilibrium, I tease, "Honky Tonk, is that a ball cap in your pocket or are you just happy to see me?"

He reaches a hand back and slides it over his lower back. The move shifts muscles that are so well defined my glands salivate. Snatching the battered hat from his pocket, he shakes it out before slipping it over his dark hair. I cluck my tongue. "Well, it's better than a Red Sox cap."

"Move it, Dancing Queen. It's going to take a while to get to the stadium and I don't want to miss the first pitch."

Since I damn well know who is playing today, I snatch up my purse and fish out my keys so I can lock up. Still, I can't help but critique his Brewers hat. "I mean, at least I know you won't be breaking into 'Turnin' Up the Heat' today."

He gives a long-suffering sigh before acknowledging the inevitable. "You're a Yankees fan."

"Do I have time to change into my Andy Pettitte jersey? My game hat?" I ask, bobbing from side to side.

"No. Get a move on . . . what the hell was that?" he asks incredulously as my exuberant movement comes to a stop.

I flush warmly. "Umm . . . nothing?"

He saunters in my direction. "Skipping and bouncing over a baseball game? That's all it takes with you?"

"I'm easy to please."

He reaches over and tugs at one of my braids before sliding his hand around the back of my neck. Hoarsely, he says, "What you are is a dream."

I think he's about to kiss me when his hand slips away. "We need to go."

"Okay," I say.

After we exit my condo, Brendan laces his fingers through mine. I could float on air. As we enter the elevator, I remark, "I had no idea you were into sports."

He nods. "I played baseball, ran track, and played soccer—though I'm forever being corrected that it's football—in high school. You?"

"Swimming, volleyball, and softball. I wasn't particularly good at any of them, but I enjoyed them."

"Same. For me, music was always my favorite. You?"

"Dance. Lots of dance until I grew too tall to be particularly good at it."

Stepping out onto the street, I whistle for a cab. By some miracle, one swings wildly in front of us. Brendan reaches for the door and holds it open so I can slide across the seat. Within seconds, we're on our way to Yankee Stadium.

Much to my pleasure, Brendan's holding onto my hand as if he doesn't mean to let it go.

It's the top of the sixth. The Yankees just scored another three runs against the Brewers and Andy Pettitte has just been subbed out by Ramiro Mendoza. I'm enjoying a sun-warm beer with have my ankles crossed on the seat in front of me when I toss out casually, "I saw my first rock concert here."

Earlier, I was pleased when Brendan took us up to the nosebleed seats. His "It's not baseball if you're not cheering your team along in the worst seats of the house" made me wholeheartedly agree. Not only that, but it was comforting to realize I could relax in the upper deck with a date as much as I could on my own.

"How long ago?"

"In the nineties."

Brendan stills. "There are exactly two shows that were played in this stadium. Billy Joel and—"

"Pink Floyd."

He lets out a low whistle. "And how did you swing that?"

"Jake begged our parents until they gave in. He was so pissed when he realized he'd have to take me instead of one of his buddies. We came down and spent the night in the city. Our parents' rules were that they escorted us to the gate and then met us right after." I take another sip of beer even though I chuckle. "That and he had to mow both family's yards without complaint for two years."

Brendan's laughter bursts out of him as sharply as the crack of the bat below us. "I'd have killed to have attended that show."

I bump his shoulder before asking, "What was yours?"

"My what?"

"Your first," I question as he lifts his beer to his lips.

He sputters the drink. "Excuse me?"

I quirk my brows and don an innocent mask. "Your first concert. Geez, Honky Tonk. What did you think I was asking?"

Then he begins to sing. Each word burns through me as Brendan's eyes hold mine while his lips form the words about being shameless.

Everything falls away as Brendan sings to me—the yeasty smell of the beer, the cheering fans, and even the heat of the sun. Enthralled as he makes each word of Billy Joel's legendary song his own. By the time he reaches the chorus, I'm ready to abandon the game.

All I want is to be with him.

After the last words fall from his lips, I whisper, "I'm not certain I could walk away from you." My words are a twist of the lyrics.

Brendan reaches for my hand but doesn't say anything for a long while.

When he does, I feel a slight chill when he whispers, "No, but you might run."

CHAPTER TWELVE

Danielle

He winked at me! And she's prettier in person!

—Ykees4EV999 (in a Yankees chat room talking about how she spotted Brendan Blake and Danielle Madison in the cheap seats at the game)

I sashay next to Brendan as we walk out of the elevator toward my front door. "Thanks for a perfect day."

He points out the stain on my shirt. "Was my hotdog shooting ketchup at you a bonus?"

I shoot him a huge helping of side-eye. "Simply a crime."

"I had no idea it would shoot that far. It's a good thing no one was sitting on the other side of you. I swear the ketchup flew four feet at least."

We look at each other and crack up. "I'll buy you a new one if you can let me know where to find a washed-out tie-dye that I don't need to make and wear myself."

The idea of stealing a worn T-shirt of his makes my nipples tingle. To hide my reaction, I taunt, "I couldn't care less about the shirt. It's the fact you committed the sin of eating ketchup on a New York City hot dog. That's the injustice I can't quite get over."

His hazel eyes dance in amusement. His voice is laced with mischief when he shares, "Are you going to find me odd if I tell you I'm also not a fan of meat on my pizza?"

We've reached my front door, but I spread-eagle to guard the entrance. "Say it ain't so."

He tugs at his lower lip before a smile spreads across his handsome features. I'm entranced by the way his beard shifts along with the planes of his face. Instead of answering, he steps closer, then braces his arm on the door to the side of me.

"Are you finally thinking about kissing me, Brendan?" I stare into his clear hazel eyes and lick my lips. That move inadvertently brushes my tongue against his lower lip.

"I damn sure planned on it." His eyes drop to my lips.

It takes everything in me to keep from trembling beneath his potent stare. "I hope you don't presume it's a sure thing."

His eyes flick upward. This close, I can see the swirls of gold and grey woven through the green. As I'm about to fall into them, he speaks. It's deep and rich, like his voice has been dunked in dark chocolate—my very favorite kind. "Nothing between us is a certainty, Danielle. That makes the need to kiss you that much stronger."

The hand closest to my head slides to the nape of my neck. His other hand slides to where my shorts and T-shirt meet. With a quick tug, his thumb rests on the skin of my hip while his fingers tug my body closer to his. "Do you want me to kiss you?"

I feel my lips part in anticipation. As many men as I've had the pleasure of kissing, I've never craved a man's lips on mine the way I do Brendan's.

"Last chance to say no," he murmurs, his mouth lowering.

My hands come to rest on his chest just as his lips cover mine. He doesn't lead me into this kiss, he plunges me into it. I feel as if my senses have just been swept up into a storm and Brendan is the only anchor.

I need to hold on, or I'm going to be swept away.

His tongue strokes over mine as one hand brushes against the smoothness of my skin. His other angles my head so when he drags his lips away, he tugs my head back as his mouth descends over the front of my throat. An anguished sound emerges from my throat at the feeling of his beard against my smooth skin.

What would it feel like in other places?

Unable to be passive when all I want to do is return every touch, every taste, I smooth one hand up his chest and around his neck until I thread it through his dark hair. With my other hand, the fingers clench against his muscular chest. I twine a leg around his hips and rock against him right as he slams me back against the door and his lips crash down against mine.

This time, there's blistering heat. Our mouths are wild against one another. I'm fighting the urge to drag Brendan just beyond the door and have my way with him on the plush carpeting.

I'm about to suggest it when the elevator dings, signaling the arrival of one of my neighbors—a proverbial bucket of ice water being thrown on us.

Brendan staggers back as if he's drunk. "What was that?"

I feel like I've been split in two by a raw pleasure I never knew could exist. After locating my ability to think, I mutter, "I think it was a kiss."

He grunts. His hands are braced on his thighs as my neighbors pass by. "Hello, Danielle."

"Hi, Mrs. Salem." I even manage to wave.

After she slips behind her door, Brendan springs at me. I find myself gently backed against the door and he's smiling from ear to ear. "If you're able to think beyond that kiss, I obviously didn't do it correctly."

I beam back at him. "It was awful. Terrible. We need more practice."

He brushes his lips against mine. "I'll give you a call tonight, Dancing Queen." Then he reluctantly lets me go.

Brendan's partway down the hall when I call out, "Hey, Honky Tonk?"

He turns around and waits for me.

"For the record, one of your shirts is enough recompense for ruining this one."

Even from this distance, his eyes begin to glow. "I'll keep that in mind."

I murmur, "See that you do," as he steps on the elevator. Once Brendan's out of sight, I step inside my condo and let out a scream of pure happiness.

CHAPTER THIRTEEN

Brendan

An American flight crew member confirmed Brendan Blake signed a Delta Kappa Epsilon fraternity flag for the Vanderbilt chapter in first class on the night flight to Nashville. "He's simply fantastic!" was gushed about the up-and-coming country musician.

—Nashville Nights

"How are things in New York?" I ask Danielle the next night.

She opens her mouth and the word that pops out isn't one I expect. "Lonely."

Before I can ask her what she means, she jokes, "My baseball partner in crime is hiding out in Nashville. It might be because his team is getting trounced in their current series."

"Listen, Dancing Queen, let's be honest." I wince at my choice of words, but fortunately she can't see me.

"Is there a time when you haven't been?" she challenges.

Only every damn minute. Instead, I drawl, "There's only one kind of baseball diamond that truly matters in this relationship."

There's a distinct pause before a loud thump, then, "Ow!"

"Danielle?"

"Give me a minute," she says with a small moan.

"What happened?" I demand.

Silence greets my answer, and my imagination goes into overdrive picturing my Dancing Queen bleeding on the floor of her condo. "Christ, why didn't I get the number of your doorman?"

"Brendan."

"God, what if you're really hurt? How in the hell do I look up the number for 9-1-1 in New York?"

"I'm not hurt," she protests.

I'm too busy frantically flipping through my Rolodex to truly hear her. I land on my buddy Beckett's name. "Listen, I think I should have one of my friends come over to make sure you're okay. Beckett's a good guy. He's not on the road this week with Small Town—"

She interrupts my frantic tirade by shouting, "Brendan, I tripped and crashed into the wall! Then I fell on my butt! No offense, I really don't want your buddy to come over and check it out."

"You fell on your ass?"

"Yes."

"Why?"

She mumbles, but I still manage to pick out the words "baseball" and "relationship."

At those words, I relax the muscles in my body one at a time—*all but one*, I think ruefully, as I cast a glance down the front of my jeans. "Let me get this straight. You fell on your ass because I inferred something sexual about our relationship?"

I hear another thunk and grin maniacally. "Dancing Queen, have you never had a man call you and leer sweet nothings in your ear?"

Danielle chortles. "Leer. Excellent choice of words, Honky Tonk."

Think I'm being funny, do you? I adjust myself in an attempt to not have my zipper imprinted on the back of my cock. "Has no one ever tried to seduce you with words, Danielle?"

Instead of picking up the bait, she answers me bluntly. "A few have tried."

Intrigued by her lack of guile, I ask, "And?"

"I find myself completely unimpressed by the whole process. Maybe that's because of what happened in the past. All I've experienced is poor attempts at men's quest for sex and no desire for anything of value."

I curse myself for being a fool. *Of course with everything that happened, she's going to think all men are like that.* Then she blows my mind. "I want a man who will look me straight in the eye and tell me his feelings, trust me to touch more than just his body."

"You're looking for love," I declare flatly.

"I'm not going to run from it. But I want his respect before I start an affair with a man. I'm a person with feelings. I have emotions. Shouldn't those come into play or is all I'm good for is as a body?" Her tone is glacial.

"It's direct."

"And it's put you off." There's a twinge of regret in her tone.

"Actually, it hasn't."

"Really?" Her voice sounds as excited as a kid in a candy store.

"I'm titillated."

"Again, an excellent choice in vocabulary. Can I ask you something?"

"What's that?"

"Where were you educated?" If Danielle were in the room, she'd realize I'd turned to stone at her innocent question. "You don't speak like a Nashville native."

I deliberately add more twang to my voice. "Aww, now, sugar. Ain't that sweet."

She's quiet for a moment before saying, "If you don't want to answer the question, just say so. There's no need to mock me."

There's an extended silence which she doesn't break. I let out a gusty sigh. "It's a touchy subject." *And one I'll never be able to tell you about.*

"And that's all you have to say. I apologize for bringing up a sensitive matter."

I stare out my window and glimpse the downtown lights of Nashville. "Dancing Queen?"

"Yes?"

"I wish you were here right now so I could hug you."

She gives a soft laugh before saying, "Are you trying to make me feel better by leering sweet nothings in my ear?"

I burst into laughter. "Damn straight."

"Good."

CHAPTER FOURTEEN

Brendan

Country music sensation Brendan Blake is heading into the studio this week with all new music. Yes, that's right. Ten new tracks will be recorded.

Studio time is his number one priority.

When will the album be released? The minute he finishes. We know his fans are clamoring for new music. We'll be expediting CD production. We expect them out no later than the end of summer.

Will they be out by his tour? We hope before that.

Yes. Any radio station that requests one will receive an advance copy.

—Wildcard Music spokeswoman Paula Stone at a press conference about Brendan Blake's new album

---

The next night, my mother and Smith come over to join us for dinner. Both kids thrive beneath my mother's doting attention and while they do, Smith and I retire to my study to talk business.

Dropping into the chair while holding my favorite guitar, I strum absentmindedly. Smith ticks off a laundry list of items I need to do in preparation for laying down tracks on my first solo album. Finally, he winds down and takes a swig from the longneck he's been holding. "Did you finalize the songs?"

I think back to the ten songs I culled from the hundreds I've written. I've sung a number of these in front of fans when I opened for Small Town Nights. A few were even included on movie scores. Then I think about dancing blond curls and blueberry-lemon pie and my fingers slide up and down the frets. I hum along until I get to the refrain. That's when I stop playing and hand him a stack of papers.

Smith reads through them and nods, likely able to feel the crowd's reaction to them as I'm singing on stage. "Have I heard any of these?"

"Nope."

"Has the label?"

"Absolutely not?"

"All new music?"

"Got a problem with that?"

"Just wondering what inspired . . . nine new songs in just a few days?"

"What else?" Before he can ask, I blurt out, "A woman."

Smith's grin widens as I keep strumming, tweaking notes and words, scribbling on a pad next to me. When I finally stop, I mutter, "No, the songs aren't quite done."

"Should I ask why you're singing about blueberry-lemon pie? Fans are going to go nuts wondering who the mystery woman is, critics will be wild with innuendos, and bakery sales everywhere are about to skyrocket."

"Hardy har har."

"You think I'm kidding? What happened when you sang 'Broken Boots' on tour with Small Town Nights?"

I open my mouth to reply but no words form. The tabloids reported that people scoured second-hand stores searching for pairs of broken in cowboy boots. Headlines like "Honky Tonk Wear Is the New Trend" and "Second-Hand Cowboy Replaces Grunge!" were on every newsstand. Frustrated, I ask, "Why can't they have just the music and not get the rest of me."

"You're kidding, right?"

I keep plucking away at my guitar. "I'm really not."

"Brendan, you chose this life." Before I can protest I didn't ask for the paparazzi, he lifts a hand. "And before you argue, you knew what you were getting into when you sang at bars in Nashville even before Kris Wilde recognized your talent. You—"

Just then, my private line rings. Once. Then she hangs up. My skin begins to tingle at the thought of hearing the sound of her voice.

His brow quirks. "Expecting a call?"

I set my guitar down in the stand before pushing to my feet. "Actually, I am. If you could tell Mom and the kids I'll be a few."

"Don't fill up on that something sweet before you get some of your mama's cooking. She's fryin' up chicken to go with the pie that was delivered today."

"Save me some and nobody had better touch that pie without me. I'm not sure how long this will be."

Now his brow is hidden by his shaggy hairline. He lets out a low whistle on his way to the door.

The phone rings again. Just as I'm about to lift the cordless receiver, I call out, "Close the door behind you!"

He shuts it smartly just as I guess who's on the other end. "You sent me another pie. And mustard. Tell me they're not meant to be eaten together."

"Good god, no. Are you kidding? That's more disgusting than the reason I sent you the mustard in the first place."

"Trying to change me, Dancing Queen?"

"Nope, just showing you the error of your ways. If you had good mustard, I figured you might stop eating ketchup on hotdogs."

I chuckle. "I'll try it, no promises. But I am curious about something."

"What's that?"

"How did you get my address?"

Danielle begins to babble. I lean back in my chair, charmed. "If you only knew what I had to go through to get the first pie to you. I had to have my agent call your label. I said that I wanted to send thank you gifts to everyone who took part in the STORM photoshoot. Then I felt bad, so I sent gifts to everyone because I felt guilty about lying, and I abhor liars."

"Did you send everyone pie?" I'd be shocked if Danielle would share her favorite sweet with everyone.

"Absolutely not. They all received lovely vases from Tiffany."

"I like the pie better."

"I thought you might. Did it taste all right?"

"I had to beat . . ." I stutter to a halt. I can't tell her about Sula and Joshua. I'm fucking up whatever this is by lying. A lie by omission is still a lie.

Exactly what she says she can't tolerate.

Shit.

"Beat?" Danielle sounds confused.

"Ahh, Smith and my mama away from it. Why do you abhor lying?"

"Jake."

"Your cousin?"

"Yes. His wife—ex, now. Thankfully. His ex-wife did a number on him. Lied and cheated on him for most of their marriage. He found out because Jenna was extremely ill one night and he couldn't reach her when he was on the way to the emergency room."

"Jenna's your niece? The one you gave the ridiculous handbag to as a gift?"

Then there's a brief silence. *This won't be good.*

"If she'd been a boy and I'd gifted her with box seats to some sporting event, would you have thought it was ridiculous?"

"Absolutely," I reply.

That gives her pause. "Really?"

"Yes." Then I decide to let her off the hook. "But if you told me those tickets were front-row seats to a concert, we'd be having a different discussion, darlin'."

Danielle hoots. "Thank you! I've been trying to make Jake understand, but nope."

"Maybe part of it is wounded pride, Dancing Queen. Maybe he wants to be the one to give his little girl those things and he can't." I think about Sula and Joshua and the lifestyle they'd have to give up if West ever grew a heart and turned over custody to me.

I can hear her nails click rapidly against a solid surface as if she's drumming them against a tabletop or a counter. "I never thought about it from that point of view."

"It's just a guess. What does the guy do for a living?"

"He's a teacher," she announces proudly.

Bingo. Just as I'm about to say something, Danielle tacks on, "A music teacher. Jake's a ridiculously talented musician. For a while, we wondered if we would have a professional musician in the family."

I jerk the phone away from my ear. "Seriously? Why did he give it up?"

She goes on to explain how old Jake was when his daughter was born and my opinion of the guy skyrockets through the roof. Blithely, she adds, "Not like any of us will let anything happen to them. They're family."

My door creaks open and Sula peeks her head inside. She raises her hand to her mouth and pretends to take a bite from a drumstick. I hold up two fingers, letting her know I'll be there in just a few minutes. She winks at me before closing the door.

I catch sight of Venus outside my window as the sun begins to set. No, it's not a star, but I make a wish anyway. If only what's true for Danielle's family were true for everyone, I wouldn't feel quite so guilty for my deception. Then I might be in a place to encourage the feelings growing for the woman on the other end of my phone.

And I wouldn't have this gnawing pit in my stomach for doing what she hates most.

Lying.

CHAPTER FIFTEEN

Danielle

Danielle Madison's bright purple eyes exploded off the cover of *Trend* this week.

We wonder if the sultry smile she aimed at the camera was for us or if she had a special Nashville native in mind while posing in the sexy Alexander McQueen ensemble?

—Models Weekly

TWO WEEKS LATER

I agreed to meet Phina at my corner Greek diner which—despite Phina's obsession with Starbucks— serves the best coffee in New York. More importantly, they don't care much about the woman sprawled in the corner booth in the back of the restaurant with a John Deere ball cap pulled low on her forehead.

I never thought I could vanish in a city the size of New York, but I'm able to do it regularly. Today, I'm grateful for the small speck of anonymity I'm offered as I hold the warm white mug between my hands.

The bell above the door jingles and my head snaps up. Phina strolls in with a much younger woman trailing behind her. The blond's hair is as curly as my own. I lean back and study the newcomer, noticing the folio in her hand and wondering who she is. *Is she a model? Nah, too short. A fashion photographer? It's possible Phina needs a second opinion.*

I don't have long to speculate. Phina drops into the booth across from me. The newcomer remains standing. Impatiently, Phina gestures her to sit down. "Dani, Emily. Emily, Dani. I thought you might like to be present for our tête-à-tête."

"Nice to meet you," I murmur, keeping my face averted.

"You too," she mumbles.

Phina takes the folio from the young woman and sets it on the table. "That wedding dress was exquisite, Emily. I'm ridiculously jealous of Naomi—the dress, not the groom."

Beneath the brim of my cap, I study Emily. A small smile creases her lips before she sasses, "I'll be happy to make you one, Phina."

"If I decide to marry for a third time, I'll hold you to it," Phina retorts as she flips open the black leather binder.

That's when I feel a disturbance in the pit of my soul as I stare down at a photograph of one of the most magnificent wedding gowns I've ever seen. "Sweet Jesus."

Emily's smile becomes infinitesimally wider while Phina begins singing the young woman's praises. "Isn't her work magnificent, darling?" A flip of a page, then "Oh! Look at this one!"

In a blink I'm halfway across the table studying a dress with the most exquisite lace I've ever seen. The dress design resembles the cape worn by Little Red Riding Hood despite its wicked sexiness. I tap a nail on the page, wondering aloud, "I've never seen this pattern of lace before, have I?"

The woman lifts her head and I get a load of deep blue eyes framed by red glasses before she declares, "That's because I designed it."

I flop back in my seat, stunned. "You designed it? The lace?"

She gives a brisk nod. "It's very versatile." Taking the book back from Phina, she flips forward a few pages until she lands on a snazzy gold dress hugging the torso of a seductive brunette modeling it. "As you see, it transforms well into a bridesmaid gown."

"Or even a formal one." I study the dress harder. "Your model looks fabulous in it."

"She has an exquisite face. It was made to be photographed," Phina agrees.

"All my models are my sisters," Emily remarks. At our incredulous expressions because each of the models are so diverse in appearance, she shrugs as an answer to our unspoken question. Neither Phina nor I press as we're more interested in the designs.

But this woman is an enigma I'd love to spend time figuring out.

I flip through the entire book, but I find myself returning to the gold dress, drawn to it by its body-hugging lines and elegance, but still . . . I tap a nail on the page. "Do you do custom designs as well?"

"All my dresses are custom-made."

Now it's Phina whose eyes bug out. "Every one? Including Naomi's wedding gown?"

"Everything, Phina. I give each of my dresses all of me."

"That's a surefire way to burn out," I challenge.

Her navy blue eyes narrow into slits. "Making Amaryllis Designs a success means only slightly less to me than my family. I give it all I've got every single day, even if I have to bleed in the process."

The words come out of my mouth before I can stop them. "I want the gold dress in black but with the neckline modified to a deeper plunge."

She shakes her head back and forth. "No, you don't."

I cock my head to the side arrogantly. "Are you sure about that?"

Emily reaches into her bag, pulls out a sketchpad, and immediately strokes bold lines. Under her fingers comes the gold dress with the swirls of lace, but instead of the modified neckline, she's raised the front hem leaving the back long. She's also added some curvature at the hips, making the wearer's waist appear minuscule. Nodding the whole time, I declare, "I approve."

"What color are your eyes?" she asks without looking up.

Phina smiles and nods. Whoever this "Naomi" is must be someone fairly well-to-do that Phina would trust Emily with my identity. I tip my hat back and drawl, "Well, they're often called purple by any number of people."

Emily's hand pauses its rapid movement for half a heartbeat. She finishes her sketch before she lifts her head from her work and sneers, "Heathens. They're not purple."

"You don't think my parents know what color my eyes are, Emily?" I'm amused rather than insulted.

She doesn't pretend not to recognize me, but it's her words that lay me out flat. "Not at all, Ms. Madison. I would hope the press has more eloquent ways to describe such a unique color. If not, it doesn't bode well for when they'll have to describe my designs. And believe me, they will."

"Confident, aren't we?" I challenge.

"Proud—of my family and my talent." While I absorb her words, she—an unknown—tutors me. "You should be saying your eyes are deep violet. That makes them dark and mysterious, just like I believe the color of this dress should be." Emily taps the end of her pencil on the sketch.

"Yes. Perfect," Phina breathes.

"I'll take it," I agree hastily, not caring about the price. Then I realize something. "Hey. Wait, what's your last name?" This girl could be simply known by her first name, for all I know.

Emily chews her lip. "Freeman. I'm Emily Freeman. Do you need that information for the contract? I have a standard one at my office I can email to you. We're on the web."

I grin at her. "No. I need to know so when I'm stopped on the red carpet, I can give them the name of my designer."

All the color drains from her face. She closes her eyes before whispering, "This is really happening?"

"Yes, Emily. It really is." Phina pats her hand.

She blinks rapidly behind her glasses before gathering herself together. Meeting my gaze head-on, she asks, "When do you need the gown completed?"

I contemplate the dresses my stylist sent over for an upcoming movie premiere and mentally dismiss all of them. I joke, "I don't suppose I could say next Friday?"

Emily doesn't blink. "Why not?"

My jaw falls open. "Are you kidding?"

"I need your measurements." Before I can interrupt her to say I'll text them to her, she continues, "Because the way this dress is designed, I need ones that aren't as simple as bust, waist, hips."

"Like what?"

She at once becomes all business. "Your armpit to hip, for one. I need to measure your biceps so the lace skims your skin but doesn't hang. I need you in heels so I can measure the distance from the floor to—"

I hold up a hand, laughing. "I get the idea."

"Use my apartment," Phina insists. "Then, if neither of you mind, I can photograph the entire process for future posterity."

It's Emily who laughs as she begins adding details to the sketch that eerily resemble my face. "Phina, I might actually believe there's such a thing as heaven if there were to come a day when a photograph of me and the legendary Danielle Madison is published."

I tap the edge of the paper Emily's casually doodling on that's becoming a magnificent piece of art with my face as the centerpiece. "If your dresses are anything like your art, that may happen sooner rather than later."

Deadpan, Emily says, "I won't let you down."

"No, you won't let yourself down."

That's when her smile turns impish. "Damn right."

CHAPTER SIXTEEN

Danielle

Danielle Madison sent back every single dress picked by her stylist for the upcoming *Crystal Palace* premiere.

Does this mean the supermodel is turning up her pert nose since she wasn't selected to be in the film?

—Los Angeles Wave

After Emily measures parts of me I didn't think were important for a dress to fit, I'm relaxing on Phina's couch. Something Emily speculated about has been chasing through my thoughts since the words popped out of her mouth a short while ago. "*If Mr. Blake is escorting you to the event, have him wear dark gray or black. If he wears blue or brown, you will clash on the red carpet.*"

If Brendan escorts me to the event. God, am I ready to share the fact we're in a relationship with the whole world?

After Emily leaves, Phina asks me gently, "Have things progressed to that point?"

"With Brendan?" I hedge.

"No, with your doorman."

I turn the glass of wine she poured me around in my hands before lifting it to my lips. "After we left the warehouse that day, I took him to dinner in Nantucket."

"Don't tell me you took him to your house as well."

I roll my eyes. "Don't be ridiculous. My family was there. I did, however, have Jake meet me at the airport with my car."

Phina's eyelashes flutter. "As beautiful as you are, your cousin is absolutely divine."

I pretend to hurl. "Please, give me a break."

"It's a pity that piece of work he was married to did such a number on him. For your cousin, I would contemplate the idea of a third marriage."

"Liar. Even if Jake were to get out of his own head long enough to lie down and sacrifice himself on an altar for you, you wouldn't go there."

"Sadly, since I could have birthed him, you're right." Her voice is forlorn.

I burst into gales of laughter. "Like that's ever stopped you before."

"It would when I know Jake is more like your brother than a distant relation. As I consider you the child of my heart, that's taking an Oedipus complex a bit too far," Phina sighs forlornly.

I snort. "Thanks. Do I owe you something for not trying your wiles on my cousin?"

"God, yes. Tell me you're going to take a chance on your own love life. Ask Brendan Blake to the premiere."

I bite my lip in consternation.

"What's holding you back? Is there something about him you haven't told me?"

I tip my head back and study the ceiling intently as I try to pull my thoughts together. Rolling my head so I meet her concerned eyes, I admit, "He could be everything I've been waiting for, Phina."

She slow blinks—in shock, I imagine. "You look like I just told you I found out that K-Mart and Alexander McQueen made a deal for producing couture gowns."

"I might believe that more easily. You've been out with him, what? Twice now?"

I nod. "Once at the island and the other here in the city."

"And after two dates, you think he could be the one?" Forgetting she's holding a stemmed glass, Phina flings her hands up in the air. Wine arcs out of the glass and onto her pristine rug. "I take it back. Go to the premiere alone. Get your head on straight."

"Phee, he—"

"I don't care how magnificent in bed he is," she shrieks, arms flapping.

"I wouldn't know," I murmur.

That stops her Big Bird impression. "Really?"

"All we've done is talk. No, that's not true. He's kissed me."

"Back it up. Those dates lasted hours, almost eight hours in one case."

"They have," I affirm.

"Whoa. He converses? Using actual words?"

"No. I have to guess what he pantomimes to me."

"Excuse me, missy. It's rare to find one of his species who knows how to say things like 'Please' and 'Thank you' let alone have a full conversation."

"In my case, they can't get past the face to the fact I actually have a mind. Brendan just . . ." I take a glug of my own drink.

"He just, what?"

I contemplate the glass in my hands. "He wants to know me. He listens. It's something so small but so overwhelming."

Phina leans over and picks up the bottle of wine from her coffee table. After topping my glass off, she takes a swig directly from the chilled green glass before declaring candidly, "If you don't ask him to the premiere, I'm having you offed so I can make a play for him myself."

Before snickering, I spit the wine I'd just sipped back into my glass. "I'm going to tell him you said that."

"When?"

Resigned, I give in. "When I ask him to the event."

Phina tips the bottle in my direction. I dutifully clink my glass against it. "Good girl."

"That's my problem."

"What?"

"When I'm around Brendan Blake, the last thing I want to be is the good girl I've always been."

CHAPTER SEVENTEEN

Danielle

Brendan Blake was spotted out this afternoon with his arms wrapped tightly around a petite brunette. Unfortunately, this journalist was unable to get close enough to get a picture.

One wonders what supermodel Danielle Madison has to say about this as the two are all the media have been speculating about since the STORM campaign.

When another media outlet asked about his "friend," Blake shot the reporter a withering glare and said, "No comment."

—Nashville Nights

Later that night, I call Brendan's private line. When he answers, a tiny puff of noise escapes my lips the second his rich baritone greets me. "Hey, Dancing Queen."

I can't help but grin at his adoption of Phina's nickname for me. "Hey, Honky Tonk."

"How was your day?" I hear something creak in the background.

"Interesting." Quickly, I summarize meeting the young designer.

He's quiet while I ramble on about the insane talent and how enamored I was of the dress, where I intend to wear it, and her surprise. When I finally run out of steam, he probes, "And she swears she can get it done in time?"

"If the measurements she took today were any indication, she's top-notch."

He hums but doesn't say anything. "Don't worry, I have plenty in my closet to wear in the event of a fashion malfunction."

At that, Brendan laughs. "Somehow, I don't doubt that." But after he says that, our conversation stalls.

For weeks, we've been talking every night regardless of where we are and not once have the calls been stilted like this one is. Finally, I blurt out, "What's wrong?"

The creaking sound pierces through the line before Brendan admits, "I'm not certain how this goes, Danielle. I've never done this before?"

"How what goes? Had a phone conversation?"

"Be serious for a moment." His voice is laced with frustration.

My spine straightens just like it used to during the years of ballet I took before my growth spurt made me too tall to become a ballerina. "Would you mind clarifying what you're getting antsy about?"

"I mean, what are we doing here?"

I recoil at the sharpness of his tone. "I thought we were having a phone conversation until apparently something crawled up your—"

He interrupts me. "I meant, are we in a place where I should assume I'm your date to this shindig? Do our publicists need to coordinate statements to the press? People are beginning to talk and I'm getting questions."

Fury building, I reply, "I see."

"Then . . .?"

"I was working my way up to it, Brendan. I'm not exactly the most self-confident person."

At that, his laughter rings over the line. "You are, quite literally, lauded as the most beautiful woman in the world and you can't find the hutzpah to ask me to escort you to the *Crystal Palace* premiere?"

"No, and that's because growing up, I towered over every boy I liked. I was teased and taunted by girls for having legs longer than some of them were tall."

His swiftly in-drawn breath lets me know he heard me. "You need to know something about me. I have feelings that get hurt just like anyone else, Brendan."

"I'm sorry, Danielle. It came out all wrong," he whispers.

"Okay," I curl into a ball or as much of one as I can with my long legs. It sparks another memory I share. "They'd invite me to help decorate at homecoming or prom. Then conveniently forget to bring the ladder."

Brendan swears ripely. "Make me feel better. Tell me your parents shove every cover you're on in their faces."

I smile wanly. "It's like you know them."

"I'd do the same thing if someone hurt . . ." He hesitates before concluding, "Someone I care for."

A warmth spreads through me.

"All this is to circle back to my apologizing for being brusque about it, Danielle."

"Why were you?"

He lets out a laugh that holds no humor. "Kristoffer Wilde asked me about you today."

"About me?"

"Someone from the Wildcard Music media department brought him a tear sheet of us at the STORM shoot."

"I won't apologize for—"

"I'm not asking you to," Brendan interrupts. "It's just . . . I've never been involved with someone from the industry before. I know how much I like you. We're just getting to know one another and suddenly Kris is tossing all these rules and reminders at me."

"Such as?" I chew my lip as I wonder if I've ever personally offended Kristoffer Wilde in some way.

"Pretty much what I flung at you—giving him and our corporate publicist a heads up if we take this public."

"Hmm."

"You don't have to do anything like that?" It might be my imagination, but Brendan sounds a bit put out.

I shrug before I recall he can't see it, me, because he's at his home in Nashville this week. "Brendan, if I do, I don't care. I'm me, always. Whether I'm at a red-carpet event, on the set, or hanging around my apartment, I'm the same woman. I don't change to suit my circumstances. What's the point?"

His heartfelt "Thank God" causes my smile to spread. I guess they worry about protecting his image because he's still relatively new to the music scene, I think. He must have a lot to lose if he doesn't play by Wildcard's rules. I'll have to ask for a list of dos and don'ts if we end up taking this further. Right now, it seems like I have my answer without having to pull up my big girl panties, but just to be sure, I ask, "So, do you wanna?"

"Do I want to what?"

"Want to walk through a million paparazzi to see what's supposed to be the hottest sci-fi flick of the summer with me? Oh, and for the record, my newest designer buddy said to only wear black or blue, or we're going to clash."

"Me or your date?"

"You. She was specific about that."

"Well, god forbid clashing should occur."

"Cardinal sin, you know."

"I know all about sinning, Danielle. Clashing doesn't come close to making the list," his seductive voice whispers in my ear.

A tingle works its way up my spine as I think about the ways I'd like to break the rules with this man. "I believe you."

"Good. And, Dancing Queen?"

"Yes?"

"It would be my honor to be the man at your side on the red carpet." I start to say thank you but then I'm stunned stupid when he continues, "But I need for you to know something important."

Hesitantly, I ask, "What's that?"

"If you'd asked me to any dance when I was a pimple-faced sixteen-year-old who pretended to have more interest in my guitar than girls, I'd have said yes then too. It has nothing to do with your looks and everything to do with who you are."

"And that is?"

He knocks me sideways when he declares, "Someone I'm free to be myself with."

"Me too. I mean, that's how I feel when I'm with you."

"So, I'm guessing I haven't botched my chance at a third date?"

Relaxing back, I cross my legs at the ankles and ask, "What do you have in mind?"

"You know I'm about to go back out on tour—just a few shows this time."

"Yes. I read about it."

"I don't want to wait to make plans to be with you again. I'm in Nashville until next week. Let's do your premiere where I promise I'll wear a black suit so we don't embarrass your little designer friend." We both laugh over Emily's impertinent instructions. Then his voice drops when he proposes, "Then I need to see more of you, Danielle. It's going to become difficult soon, but I don't want to lose this connection between us."

"Me too."

"Then let's take this one date at a time."

"I can work with that."

"I'm in New York a few weeks after your event. Dinner? Movies? Maybe a show?"

"Yes, to all of that, Brendan." Meanwhile, my heart's pounding out of my chest. *He wants to be with me!*

"Maybe you could come hear me play?"

There's a pregnant pause after he casually lays out his invitation, but we both know there's nothing casual about it. I reiterate to make certain I didn't misunderstand. "Play? As in, come see you on the road? But none of your shows are in New York."

"Yet. That's a pretty big word you forgot there," he tacks on, momentarily distracted.

"Yet," I repeat softly. "I have no doubt you'll be selling out stadiums soon, Brendan."

A hint of vulnerability seeps into his voice. "Do you really think so?"

"One day, when my face is but a memory, your words will continue to be sung with reverence." I'm not blowing sunshine up his ass; it's just the truth about the differences between our two industries.

"I've barely begun to climb the ladder and you're at the pinnacle of yours. How you can say something like that is beyond me."

"Flattery," I proclaim, "will get you anything you want."

"Including you in the wings while I'm on stage?"

"If you're certain."

"I'm never more myself than when I'm performing. I love I've been privy to some pretty deep parts of you. Let me give you the heart of me."

"Then my answer is yes." Until Brendan said that I didn't realize I had opened myself up to him. Didn't realize that was my intent. Now that he's reflected my actions back to me, I want the same from him. No, I need it.

I have to know all the facets of this man before I fall all the way in love with him. After Jake's tangled web of lies, love terrifies me more than posing nude. It exposes so much more than my skin.

It lays my heart bare.

His voice is smug. "Then it's settled. You and me, Dancing Queen."

"I love the way that sounds."

"Me too. And, Danielle?"

"Yes?"

"Next time I'm not stopping with just a kiss."

Envisioning Brendan's body over mine, I reply breathlessly, "That sounds perfect."

PERFECTLY FREE

CHAPTER EIGHTEEN

Brendan

Wildcard Music lied.

They said Brendan Blake was working on new music. What they didn't say is he was working on what may be country music's Record of the Year.

Even before the full CD is out, Wildcard released the first single from the album, "Blueberry Pie."

Blake may be hitting stardom sooner than he expected. "Blueberry Pie" is quickly climbing the

charts to challenge Train, Alicia Keys, and Lifehouse for the year's top single.

—Los Angeles Wave

"Love the new tracks, Brendan," my drummer Carson calls out.

Gil, the house keyboardist, snickers. "Don't even try to deny that this song is about a woman, man."

I don't acknowledge either of them as I slip the headphones back over my ears and face the clear glass wall that separates the booth from the studio. I lean into the microphone and ask Dusty, "How was the last recording?"

He shakes his head before his voice reverberates in my headphones through the talkback system. "I want to hear you play it, B. Just you. Carson can listen and suggest what he thinks needs to be added for rhythm."

Since Dusty produced Small Town Night's album, I trust his instincts. I relay the instructions to the guys in the room before dragging a stool up to my mic. Doing a quick strum to make certain I'm still in tune, I wait for the countdown before I start. "You swore I'd remember this night . . ."

The rest of the song flows out of me. I'm so caught up in laying down the lyrics I have no idea what Carson's doing behind me.

After I strum the last note, there's silence before both rooms erupt in wolf whistles and applause. I remove my headphones just as Dusty slams open the studio door announcing, "And Blueberry Pie is in the can. That was sheer perfection, man. The world is going to go nuts."

I slide from my stool so quickly I almost topple over the mic stand in front of me. Making a quick grab for it sets off a screech that has everyone but me covering their ears. After I right the mic, the awful noise stops. "Are you serious?"

"Not if you end it by knocking over my equipment," Dusty grimaces.

"Dusty." My voice is impatient.

"Listen and draw your own conclusion. As for me, this is the cut that should go on the album. Hell, I think it should be the first single."

My eyes widen fractionally at his words, knowing he's likely to pass them along to Kristoffer Wilde. "Give me one sec." Dusty returns to his boards while I quickly slide my guitar strap over my head and place it in the stand. After I put the noise-canceling headphones back on, I signal Dusty before speaking into the mic. "I'm ready."

Chills race through me as I hear my voice reminisce about my first date with Danielle. My heart skips when Gil and Carson provide backup, harmonizing at just the right moment before edging out to let this be about me and the blueberry pie I'd always have a craving for.

My fans are going to have a lifelong fascination with this song, much like I fear I'm starting to experience with the woman I wrote it about.

Shoving thoughts about Danielle out of my head, I agree with the people in the room who are eagerly awaiting my judgment. "You're right. It's everything we wanted it to be."

A cheer goes up. The first song of ten is recorded. I'm ecstatic—of course I am. Clenching my jaw, I refuse to admit I had a chance to call Danielle to let her know.

CHAPTER NINETEEN

Danielle

Long distance rates have increased slightly and long-distance companies are finding other ways to increase customer costs as well, according to Consumer Action's 2001 Long Distance Rates Survey of 19 carriers and 44 discount calling plans.

Industry leaders AT&T, MCI-WorldCom, and Sprint (the Big Three) usually adopt a follow-the-leader approach to policy changes. Since last year, basic rates at AT&T and MCI-WorldCom increased during evenings and weekends by up to 13%.

—ConsumerAction

"Hello?"

"Danielle." Just my name, but the sound of it on his lips after I've tasted him sends shivers coursing through my body.

"Brendan." Is that my voice all raspy?

"What were you doing?"

"Thinking about you." Then, damn it, I knock my shampoo into the tub. It lands with a splash.

His voice is deeper when he asks, "What are you doing?"

Honest as ever, I tell him, "Taking a bath."

"Christ, Danielle. You're hell on a man's control."

My breath lifts my breasts above the waterline and exposes them to the cool air. My nipples tighten and cause more sensitive areas to tingle. I slink deeper into the water and curse myself for picking up the phone. "Maybe I should call you back?"

"Or maybe I should tell you how I wish I was there."

I bite my lower lip. "Or you could do that."

"Do you know how much I want to lift those curls and let my lips drift over the curve of your shoulder while I soap your breasts from behind?"

My walls contract slightly at the imagery his words paint. "No. I didn't think about it until just now." *Probably because I was wrapping my mind around the idea of absorbing you into my body,* I admit silently.

My legs shift restlessly against one another. The water sloshes. I know Brendan can hear it because his voice is way sexier when he taunts, "If I didn't still have the taste of your mouth burned on my brain, I think you were teasing me, Danielle."

"No! That's not true," I protest weakly. "I'm not some femme fatale."

"You're not? You're only the most beautiful woman on the planet."

"That's only skin deep."

"I won't lie and say what's on the outside doesn't attract me to you. It does. But the same woman who dances on a whim and wears pigtails when she—"

"I'm wearing them right now," I blurt.

He swears ripely.

"That . . . turns you on?"

"Danielle, you smile at me, and I turn hard as stone. You laugh, and I feel my insides quicken. When I imagine you doing what I think you're doing, I want to punch my hand through a wall."

"What do you think I'm doing?" I ask wonderingly.

"Touching yourself while thinking about me," he challenges.

"Brendan. I'd be lying if I said I didn't"—he groans loudly in my ear, but I rush on—"touch myself."

"Do you think about me?"

"That's a bit personal." My cheeks are warmer than the bathwater. I might increase the temperature of my bath if I stay on the phone with this man.

"Because I think about you."

My breath catches in my throat.

"I more than think about you, Danielle."

This time, my gasp can't be muffled, but then a rueful laugh immediately follows. "I guess I did ask for honesty, didn't I?"

I can practically see the grin slash across his face. "You did. So, have you . . .?"

I reach for my wine glass and take a quick hit before setting it back on the floor with a clink. My hand has a slight tremor as I smooth it over the soapy skin covering my breasts. "Who says I'm not right now?"

He mutters, "You're not kidding."

"No." My hand drifts across my abdomen, skimming the top of my thighs.

"If I were there, would you show me how to touch you?"

"If you were here, I think you'd know how to touch me better than I know how to do it myself," I admit with complete candor.

"You might be right." His voice drops lower just as I'm about to let that arrow pierce my heart. "Cup your breast for me, my queen."

I start to before almost dropping the phone in the tub. I fortunately catch it in time. "I almost drowned you."

"Christ, we need to be together to try this in the water."

I fervently agree.

Brendan growls sexier than I've ever heard him. "Bath time's over, sweetheart."

"Ex—excuse me?" I stammer.

"Time for me to tuck you in."

Now I have to clench my thighs together, imagining what will happen when I call him back from my bed, where I already dream about him. Breathlessly, I say, "Give me a few minutes?"

"I'll give you as long as you need," he whispers before disconnecting the call.

Lying back against the tub, I know my choice has been made. And not just about resuming my call with Brendan tonight.

About my future.

CHAPTER TWENTY

Danielle

IS BRENDAN BLAKE'S INTEREST IN WILLOWY BLONDES WANING?

A local deli manager claims country's number one crooner was out for lunch with a "young stunner. Remarkable eyes."

The manager shook his head when pressed if they were the purple eyes of Danielle Madison. "Can't say it was."

—New York Entertainment

I'm standing several stories above the streets of Manhattan as Phina takes a few photos of me before Brendan arrives for the premiere.

"Whatever you're thinking of right now, don't lose that look," Phina orders.

I would be hard-pressed not to be thinking of Brendan right now. I keep that thought to myself as Phina circles around me, snapping away as Jamal touches up my makeup a final time. Curious, I ask, "Do you ever think there will be a time you'll actually use these photos or do you just enjoy taking them?"

The mad clicking pauses briefly when Jamal's laughter rings out. Phina snickers. "I'm just preparing for your future, darling."

"No one can know what the future holds." The sudden peal of the doorbell traps whatever else I was about to say inside my head.

It doesn't stop Phina's murmur as Jamal makes his way over to let Brendan in. "True, which is why I'll do my best to help you remember the past later."

His deep rumble has relegated Phina to the back of my mind as I glide away from the window. He crosses through my foyer into my living space seconds later. His eyes widen fractionally before they roam from the crystals woven in my hair to my Swarovski-encrusted Stuart Weitzman sandals. As his eyes take their time journeying over me, singeing off the clothes Emily worked so hard to complete on time, I practically drool over his broad shoulders and narrow hips in the black tux he donned for the occasion.

Phina and Jamal blow me a kiss as they slip out the front door. I shoot them a small wave from my hip as they slip out my front door leaving me alone with Brendan.

A Brendan I've never seen before.

Watch out Pierce Brosnan, Brendan Blake may take over your role as 007.

Brendan exudes an unparalleled masculine sensuality in his evening clothes. But regardless of what he wears, every time I'm in the same room with him, the connection between us deepens. *This man could be very dangerous to the foundation of your heart, Danielle. Tread carefully.*

This wasn't part of the plan when I first invited him to be a part of STORM. I wanted to unobtrusively thank him for not making me another statistic, for being a good man. I didn't expect the price I'd pay to be my heart. Fear begins to trickle in—not of the man, but of my own feelings. *I didn't expect to lie awake in bed counting the stars until I fell asleep thinking of him.*

Dreaming of him.

Of us.

Of the ways we could be.

"Danielle, this is your last chance," Brendan offers reluctantly.

That snaps me from my reverie. "Last chance?"

"To walk down the red carpet alone." He circles around me and lets out a low whistle. "You're going to outshine everyone at this event."

"Brendan, I want you with me." Suddenly, it strikes me, and my voice cracks, "Unless you've changed your mind. I . . . get it. It's . . ." Before I can finish the rest of the sentence, Brendan's arm snakes out and he yanks me to him.

I crash against his chest. *I was made to be in his arms,* is my first thought when the length of my body rests against the muscles of his.

Something similar must cross his mind because his voice is even deeper when he tries to explain, "The last thing I want to do is dim your shine."

Pressing my hands against his lapels, I contradict, "You won't. You can't."

"In comparison to you, I'm a nobody."

"We're both nobody except who we are to each other. The rest of the world . . ." I flap my hand to indicate how much they matter.

Up close, I'm privy to the deep green spiking the light silvery gray color of his eyes as my words penetrate. His whisper skates along my spine, causing goose bumps to rise beneath the dark violet lace. "Danielle, I haven't been entirely upfront about who I am."

Fear causes my body to tremble. Still I'm glad my voice is steady when I ask, "About?"

"There's a part of me I can't share with you. I won't discuss it, nor will I apologize for it."

He holds me loosely, ready to let me go if I decide it's too much. I reason out the obvious. "You're not married."

He shakes his head but offers no more explanations. Nothing in our previous dates nor in any of our conversations has led me to believe he hasn't—no, won't—share the truth with me over time. "Tonight's not the night for anything other than the fact our names are about to be linked together publicly. If this . . . whatever we are . . . goes the distance, it could affect you."

I ignore the ache he's generated by being unable to define what we're becoming to one another and instead focus on something I can address. "I knew that going in."

"You don't know everything about me."

"And you don't about me." There's silence after my statement while he absorbs what I'm saying. "Brendan, I could have an addiction to collecting Q-Tips. Maybe I have a flatulence problem when I'm anxious."

He cringes, as expected. "Stop. Those things are seriously gross."

"I grew up with Jake. I swear he had those habits."

Brendan laughs. His thumb runs over the cord of my throat before resting on my pulse. "I don't want you hurt."

"And you don't think Jake farting in a bathroom and locking me in didn't hurt?" I feebily joke.

"Danielle." He murmurs my name in such a way I sober immediately.

"It's one night."

"It's a beginning," he corrects me.

"Stop borrowing trouble," I chastise.

"I can't help it. I'm too used to protecting those I care about. And you, Danielle, are becoming one of those people. Even if it means staying away from you for your own good."

It's a clue, but one I'm not up to dissecting right now. "It's my life, and you don't get to take my choices away, Brendan. While I thank you for caring, I disagree."

"Danielle," he starts.

"People wax poetic about dancing in the rain when the reality is they spend their time afraid of getting wet. You're worth the storm."

His hand slides up to cup my nape. Eyes intense, he hisses, "Keep saying stuff like that, and you'll make not falling for you an impossibility, Danielle."

Really? I'm certain I think the word, but Brendan's soft smile lets me know I must have squeaked it.

He steps back and holds out an arm. "Last chance."

I snatch my clutch off the end table before slipping my arm through his. "I'm ready."

He must read the strength of conviction in my actions. He tips my face up with his free hand and brushes my lips with his. "You're more than that. You're perfect for me. Everything about you. If I . . . Shit. Look at the time!"

Right now, just as his words were getting interesting, I resent the premiere. I despise our conflicting schedules. I want—no, need—some time with Brendan to untangle this mess of feelings twisting us up into a knot.

CHAPTER TWENTY-ONE

Danielle

Danielle Madison walked into the premiere of
Crystal Palace wearing a dark violet gown that is
obviously custom-made. The amaryllis flowers and
entwined vines lace pattern—a beautiful work of art
—suited the long limbs of the graceful supermodel.

When asked about the designer, she proclaimed,
"Emily Freeman of Amaryllis Designs." After a
quick twirl that sent the incredible lace aflutter,
Madison giggled, "It's my first original design.

Emily knocked it out of the park."

It should be noted most of the world will be focused on the fact the man at her side, country music's newest sensation Brendan Blake, was wearing a black Gucci tux.

—Los Angeles Wire

The location of the red carpet, set alight by star power and flashbulbs, can be seen in the distance a few blocks away. As the driver merges into the long line of cars waiting to unload hordes of celebrities, I give Brendan his final out. "You don't have to leave the car if this goes against some relationship code you adhere to."

His eyes narrow on me, but he waits on my next outburst of words.

"I mean, I don't want you thinking I'm going to cling too tightly. I invited you because I thought . . ."

"Shut up, Dancing Queen."

My mouth flaps open and shut like a fish before I shout, "How dare you tell me to shut up!"

The damn man just laughs. "And there she is. I've been waiting for her to show up since we left your condo."

"You essentially told me you didn't want to be here with me."

"No, I—" Brendan is interrupted by the limo driver as he exits, leaving Brendan and me alone for a few precious seconds. "Danielle, this isn't the time or place."

"It is if you don't want to be here." I bat my lashes sweetly.

"I only want to be with you!" The silence that follows that eruption is just a prelude to another explosion. Only it's not riddled with frustration but with yearning when he admits, "I hear your voice, and my pulse quickens. I look at you, and I'm blinded. What will happen if I let you into my life any further?"

"Brendan, look at me," I order quietly.

Jaw clenched, he does.

And just like I'm beginning to suspect it does for him too, my world disappears except for him. I reach blindly for his hand. When I finally latch onto it, I lift it to my face. "We'll work through this together. I don't know what to do. All I can say is I'm fumbling through this as much as you are."

His fingers caress my jawline before he admits, "I don't want you hurt."

In his eyes, I see everything I've waited for in a man: honesty, respect, and devotion. And I tell him what I wholeheartedly believe. "You won't hurt me intentionally."

His voice is jagged. "That will never happen. I will never hurt you with intent. I . . ." His lips clamp down before he can say anything else as the driver opens the door. The screaming of the crowd is just beginning to edge up, wondering who the next celebrity to emerge might be.

And Brendan's wound up tighter than a racehorse in the start gate.

Before he can launch from the limo, I touch his shoulder. He whips around, asking, "Is everything okay?"

I brush my lips against his, a whisper of a touch. "I just wanted to thank you for escorting me."

The tension releases from his body. He falls back against the seat and studies my outfit for just a moment. Then his lips twitch in the corners as he informs me seriously, "It's a good thing you found a new designer. She doesn't make you look like a hag, as some of the others do."

I'm sputtering with laughter as Brendan winks before sliding out of the car. The sound of screams ratchets up a notch. I hear several "Brendan!" and "I love you!" as well as at least one "Marry me!" over the rest of the indistinct screaming.

I call out to get his attention. "Well now, isn't this fun, Honky Tonk?"

He ducks his head back in, presumably to assist me from the car. His cheeks are flagged with color. "You knew this would happen."

"I might have had an idea," I admit.

"I'm going to make you pay for that," he says, then holds out a hand.

I place mine in his. It's more than a gesture of assistance. It's one of trust and faith. Seconds after he helps me alight from the vehicle, he tucks me up against his body. Immediately, we're engulfed by flashing lights and screaming fans. We pose for a second before making our way between the line of flashing bulbs.

We're just about to stop to talk to a reporter when Brendan leans over and whispers in my ear, "When I finally slide this gorgeous dress away from your body, I'm going to make you beg for my cock, Danielle. Think about that as you try to answer questions from the media and fans."

Damn him, now I can think about nothing else. I have to force myself to drop Emily's name with each and every fashion outlet, giving the designer her due. Because, since Brendan's all but promised to rip the dress from my body as soon as he can, this dress may never again see the light of day.

Hours later, we've just finished chatting with Roger Stephens, star of *Crystal Palace*, who made us laugh hysterically with his quick-witted humor. "How do you know him so well?" Brendan asks as he steers us away from the megastar.

"When I first came to the city, I used to watch him at open mic nights before he was discovered in a huge way." We've been here for hours and I'm beginning to wonder if, despite his protests, Brendan came to see and be seen.

His next words dissipate any doubts that crept into my mind. "Is it just me, or do you feel like you don't belong here? I'm done with posturing." His eyes blaze into mine. "I only want to be with you."

"You do?" I'm impressed I manage to keep my voice level.

His arm tightens around my waist before his voice rasps, "This has been fun, but it's empty pleasure. The feelings you churn up in me are anything but that."

The long, delicious shiver his words cause makes my voice choppy when I admit, "The best part of my day is talking to you."

"My dreams fill with you, Danielle. They're consumed by you."

"What do you dream of?"

"Naughty girl for asking here when I can do fuck all about it," he rasps. Then he leans over and whispers, "I dream of draping those long legs over my shoulders and feasting on your pussy until you beg me to let you come. Then, after you cry out, I surge inside your body. And just as my cock sinks inside you, with your heels digging into my back, I fucking wake up."

I trail my fingers up his arm. "And after the first time?"

He lets out an expulsion of air. "Goddamn, Danielle."

I stare into his eyes and deliberately throw more gasoline onto the fire. "Have we spent enough time here?"

He doesn't reply, at least not with words. Carefully, he lifts my champagne glass from my hand and passes it to a waiter before clasping my hand and tugging me from the room. Once we clear the loudest part of the party, he mutters, "I hope like hell the limo is waiting."

"There are cabs waiting at the side entrance."

Brendan course corrects, obviously in a hurry to get us away from the party and in each other's arms.

I couldn't approve more.

CHAPTER TWENTY-TWO

Danielle

It wasn't long after Roger Stephens wowed the world at the *Crystal Palace* premiere that two of its most noticeable attendees were marked absent—Danielle Madison and Brendan Blake.

The duo was spotted slipping out the side door of the theater into one of New York's plethora of cabs. Unfortunately, the driver quickly merged into traffic, stopping anyone who tried to follow them.

Where were they going that they needed to leave amid the after party? Did Danielle's dress have a malfunction that only Brendan could fix?

—Models Weekly

Brendan's molded to my side while we ride in the cab back to my building. His fingers trail over my crossed legs, sending rioting emotions through my body.

Fear and arousal are vastly different, yet they both have the capability of robbing us of the ability to speak.

I know I should be talking to Brendan about what's about to happen, but I can't. If I do, would he refuse to touch me? Figure out a way to escape from drowning me with the fiery pleasure burning in the back of his eyes since he saw me earlier?

Will I ever know what it's like to take a man into my body?

His thumb slides over the silk of my hose, the callouses catching slightly. Cognizant of the cabbie just a few feet away, Brendan leans over and whispers into my ear, "Do you know what seeing you in that dress has done to me tonight?"

I shake my head. My skin is so sensitized. The long curls that brush my shoulders tantalize my skin just as much as the puff of air Brendan leaves on them before he wrecks my updo by plucking away the few strategic pins holding it in place. Once my curls have cascaded over his fingers, he fists his hand through them.

"It's done this." Without warning, he tips my head back and begins devouring my lips.

The angle of the kiss, nor its location, is comfortable for me. But Brendan more than gets his point across—he wants me. Soon. Now.

The minute we pull to the curb, he's flinging bills at the driver and hauling me out of the cab to the sidewalk. When he straightens, we're exactly the same height. It's something small, but it recovers my equilibrium about this being right—about Brendan being the right man.

I lean forward and wrap my arms around him, pressing my forehead against his. "I've never wanted anyone the way I want you."

A truth.

"Fuck." He yanks me close and tastes me again. Perhaps the biggest truths we'll share are without words. Maybe they're only exchanged when we're wrapped in each other's arms.

He pulls back from the kiss, his hands rubbing up and down my arms. "Do you want me to stay, Danielle?"

I have to tell him. "Brendan."

"Invite me to stay," he presses.

"It's not that easy."

"It is. It's exactly that easy." His hands cup my face, forcing my eyes to meet his. "We walk into that building, then we'll enter your home. At which point, I'll strip every piece of this tantalizing dress from your skin. When I have you naked, I plan on spending my time worshiping every inch of your skin with my lips . . ."

"I've never done this before," I blurt.

The air between us stills as my words hover in the air. "What the hell do you mean?" An edge laces his voice now. "Never had a hotdog loving . . ."

I shove away from him and hiss, "Damn you, Brendan. Don't ruin it. You'll. Be. The. First. And if you can't handle that, then get the hell away from me."

His eyes flare, but his expression is blank. And right now, I hate him as much as I want him. He doesn't say a word either way. My cheeks flame in embarrassment. "I should have kept my damn mouth shut," I curse myself before I spin away.

I get maybe two steps before he catches my arm in his grip. Brendan's expression is still blank, but his eyes are molten, the hazel almost fully eclipsed by his pupils. His voice is barely audible when he guides me past the night guards. "If you'd waited, your ass would have been red from me spanking it, Danielle. That's not something you drop on a man when he's so aroused he could hurt you."

Sarcastically, I fling at him as we enter the elevator, "The next time I happen to mention my chaste status to a man, I'll be sure to . . ."

I don't get a chance to finish the sentence. Brendan has me pushed up against the wall of the elevator, stealing the words from my lips. His tongue strokes against mine, fanning the desire I have for him higher. I know by the time we reach my floor, he's going to lay waste to any chance I have of not begging for him to take me.

The elevator slows and Brendan drags me out of it. I stumble and jerk my arm back. Just as I bend over to unbuckle the heels I've been wearing, Brendan pulls me in front of him before backing me into the wall. Raising my skirt slightly, his smile turns lazy. "Hop up, my queen. I haven't properly courted you."

My lips part slightly. My arms slide around his shoulders just as his cup my rear. "You can't be serious."

Then I give a yelp when Brendan boosts me up against the wall so I'm looking down into his face. "Can't I? I promise not to drop you."

Now or always? The thought flits through my mind, but I shove aside everything but tonight. My legs wrap around Brendan's lean hips. A shudder wracks his body, and he presses himself against my core for just a moment. My head clunks back against the wall.

He grits out. "Not like this. Your place. Now." And he turns to stalk down the hall with me clinging to him. Each step he takes rubs his cock against my core. Every jostle amps up my arousal—something I wonder if Brendan can feel through my lingerie. I bury my face in his neck in embarrassment just as we reach my apartment. Setting me on my feet, I'm turned to face the door.

"Key?" he demands from behind me.

I fiddle with my clutch and open the door before he ushers us both inside. The snick of the lock followed by his hands resting on my shoulders causes me to shudder with relief. Tossing my purse on the couch, I spin around, only to be swept into Brendan's embrace. His lips cover mine, tongue pushing past any token resistance.

We're both beyond the point of refusal, of denying one another what we most need—each other. When our kiss ends, I gasp, "I've waited a long time, Brendan."

His eyes bore into mine. "Why did you?"

"I wanted it to mean something."

"And you think it will with me?"

I nod before I take his hand and lead him to my bedroom, stopping at the edge of my bed.

"I may end up breaking your heart, Danielle." His lips trail down my neck. My body melts into his as he reaches around and feeds each of the small buttons through their loops. He presses a hard kiss to the base of my throat as the top of my dress starts to give way. "I won't make any promises."

I tilt his chin up so I can stare directly into his eyes when I give him my reassurance I know what I'm doing. "I know."

Just then, my dress falls to the floor. Exposing the scraps of lace I've been wearing underneath.

"God, help me. There's no way I can stop touching her," he groans. His fingers reach out and gently trail over a painfully tight nipple. It's like lightning, causing my stomach to clench and heat to build between my legs.

"I don't think God's here right now," I sass as I shove his tux jacket over his shoulders and attack his tie.

Brendan stills my movements while he quickly sheds his cufflinks and a few studs before hauling his shirt over his head. He then releases the front catch of my strapless bra before holding my hands away from my body when I'd have covered it up. Brendan groans, "If he isn't, at least he left a work of art in his place."

With those sweet words, he pushes me until I flop backward on my bed and he's made a place for himself in between my thighs. After making quick work of my heels and stockings, Brendan reaches for the scrap of material covering my sex. I flinch.

Now I'm in unfamiliar territory, I joke with myself mentally, even as I tremble beneath his soothing fingers as they trail a pattern over my skin.

His smooth voice, rough with the passion filling the air, whispers, "Give me all of your gift, my queen."

With those words, I can't deny him. I lift my hips as he tugs the wisp of material away from my core. But instead of feeling scared, I feel something different once Brendan's eyes feast on me.

Treasured.

His hand, rough against my skin from the years of playing guitar, drags over my skin, leaving not an inch unexplored. I arch into his touch like a cat. His eyes darken. "Touch yourself, Danielle. Imagine it's my hands on you."

"Wh-what will you be doing?" I stammer as my hands skim over the bedsheets toward my breasts.

Brendan throws me a lazy smirk before he drops to his knees.

I let out a strangled cry when I felt his beard touch the inside of my thighs. Immediately, my hands fly to my small chest. The skin is so sensitive and my back arches. Then again, that might be because Brendan's found my core.

His eyes gleam at me from in between my thighs, a place he arrived at by licking and nipping his way. I'm a writhing mess. "Brendan," I plead. There's no way he can understand the intense throb building inside of me, I'm certain of it.

I ache in ways I never knew were possible, ways I never knew of when I touched myself in the dark thinking of him.

"Do you know what I'm dying to do to you, Danielle?"

"Wh-what?"

"Ah, darlin'. It might be simpler to show you." He lowers his head and nips at my swollen bud.

I almost levitate off the bed. "Ahh!"

That damn devil smirks again right before he tucks my clit into his mouth and sucks on it. My back arches as he kisses it, masterfully and mercilessly. When Brendan's fingers slide through my wetness into the core of me, I'm too far gone to feel anything but hungry. I writhe against his mouth, bucking my hips up against his lips to get closer.

"Damn, Danielle. This pussy is going to be the death of me," he groans. The vibration of that sound just agitating me further.

"Please," I beg him.

"Just a little more," he promises. His fingers are dragging in and out. His head is about to lower again, but I shove my hands through the thick mass of hair and yank.

Hard.

Panting, I gasp, "I need you, Brendan."

His forehead presses against my thigh before I feel the nod. Standing, he fishes his wallet out of his slacks. Sliding out a foil packet, he holds it in between his teeth while he toes off his dress shoes and socks, and bends over to push down his slacks and briefs. When he stands up straight, he's naked.

Fully naked.

Magnificently naked.

Without breaking my gaze, he tears open the condom packet and rolls it on before he crawls onto the bed in between my thighs. Still on his knees, he uses one hand to drag his cock through my wetness, ensuring he's well lubricated. The other alternates between plucking my nipples, circling my clit, and grazing over my entrance—keeping me at the same heightened level I was at while he devoured me.

Breaking from his delicious torture, he catches me with his hand behind one knee. "Around my back," he orders before falling forward on that hand, still holding his cock at the base with his other one.

I've seen enough movies to get the idea. With a hushed whisper, I ask, "Both of them?"

He nods, then says, "Are you sure, Danielle? Last chance. There's no going back."

I tilt my hips to brush against his shaft to answer him. He shudders. Slowly he eases forward. At first, I stare as the head pushes into my body, but I can't watch. Instead, my eyes raise to find Brendan's peering at me.

He trembles. "I've never done this before."

"Liar," I scoff.

Something deep and dark flashes in his eyes before a tidal wave of sensuality crashes over me as he pushes even deeper. It's intense, and full, so much pressure that I gasp.

"You're my first virgin, Danielle." He pushes forward a little more before pulling back. I'm panting, wanting to feel him inside me. I open my mouth to tell him just that when he steals my words with his own. "I don't want to hurt you."

He pulls back and I whisper, "If you do, you'll make it up to me."

His eyes kindle. "Damn straight I will."

With that, he surges forward and I clamp down on him. Every part of me—arms, legs, and the muscles of my inner channel—spasms around Brendan. After a few moments of holding himself perfectly still, he whispers the only word I didn't know how much I'd need to hear in this moment. "Perfect."

Then he kisses me. I can taste myself on him, which sets off something wild and wicked inside me. I score my nails over Brendan's back as he slowly begins to rock his hips. My head falls back and he trails his lips over my exposed neck as his thrusts intensify.

And I'm not so naïve that I don't know what we're chasing.

My body's hypersensitive with his body thrusting over mine. The feel of his cock stretching the tissue of my core. I kiss Brendan, and then I drag a hand from his back so I can lick my finger. He snarls, "No. Mine." Then he captures the digit in his mouth, sucking it before releasing it with a pop. Through it all, he maintains the steady pace that's driving me wild.

But I'm about to push us over.

I drop my finger to my clit and gently touch that bundle of nerves. Whether it's because it's the combination of Brendan and me, my head snaps back as I gasp. "Bren—"

He thrusts deeper. Harder. "Go. Fucking. Over."

I rub myself once more and I fly. I'm not certain where the sounds come from—me? Brendan? But as my hips lift into Brendan's I clench around him as if that's what my body was built to do.

He pistons inside me a few more times before he collapses on top of me.

Since I just ran a marathon, stopped a moving train, and completed a photoshoot—at least that's how much energy I feel like I spent—I pat Brendan on the shoulder before my head flops to the side, exhaustion pulling me under.

I'm not sure how much later it is when I feel Brendan slide out of me. He's peppering kisses all over my face, but it's his words that make my heart clench. "I hope you never regret giving me that gift."

And as I drift off, his magnificent voice sings me the most perfect lullaby.

An '80s love ballad.

CHAPTER TWENTY-THREE

Brendan

Country music star Brendan Blake was spotted having an intimate dinner with supermodel Danielle Madison at Tavern On the Green. Judging by the number of comments on social media, neither of their fans are happy the two seem to be making a love match.

—New York Entertainment

Hours later, when Danielle shows signs of life, I quickly sprint to the kitchen and yank out the most celebratory item I could find in her refrigerator.

Ice cream.

Snagging it and two spoons, I hurry back into the bedroom and slide back into the bed with the woman who has completely addled my brain. When her eyes flicker open, I hold out a spoonful of Chunky Monkey and say the first thing that comes to mind. "Thank you."

She opens her mouth, sparking images of other things I'd like to teach her. *Down, Blake. You just took her like she was a seasoned veteran at this. She's got to be sore,* I admonish myself. Eyes sparkling, she reaches for the other spoon and fills it with a good size bite. Holding it up to my lips, she wonders, "Shouldn't I be saying that to you?"

I bend down and kiss her. Her lips are cool—completely opposite of the heat at the core of the woman. Then I gobble up the ice cream she's offering. "Nope. It was my gift. Mine to cherish."

She blushes and I can say with one hundred percent certainty that supermodel Danielle Madison literally blushes from head to toe. "I'm glad you accepted it the way it was intended."

I scoop another bite into her mouth and let her swallow. My dick twitches at the way the ice cream slides down her throat. I scrub a hand over my face. Christ, I need to stop thinking about sex. "I wouldn't want to misinterpret."

Her head cocks to the side. "You think there's a reason beyond the fact I'm just selective."

"Yes," I declare bluntly.

She jabs the spoon back into the ice cream. Placing it in my mouth, she relents, "You're right."

That's when Danielle explain how so many high-powered individuals in the modeling industry, "men and women, Brendan, find it acceptable to use sex as a bartering tool."

"That's disgusting."

"And why I embraced my sexuality by holding it close. It was my *decision* who I gave myself to. I wasn't going to capitulate because of a job, nor was I going to let myself be taken by force."

My head ducks. "I hope you feel you made the right choice."

"Without question."

My head snaps up to find her grinning at me. "So, in a way, you've rescued me more than once."

"Is that all I am to you, Danielle?" I inquire silkily.

Her mumbled, "I didn't say that," reaches my ears and sets my heart thumping in my chest.

I tuck a piece of hair away from her face. "Danielle, it could have been very painful for you if you hadn't spoken up. I might not have been as careful with as hungry as I was for you."

"And I was afraid you'd stop if you knew."

My hand reaches across the sheet, palm up. "It was a shock, yes. But it felt right in the sixty seconds I had for it to settle. And it's a secret, beyond that of lovers. It's something that will forever link us."

Her hand reaches for mine. Her plump lips part before a hushed "It will?" emerges.

I bend over her hand and kiss her fingers. "Yes, my queen."

There's a stillness between us before Danielle muses, "If you ever happen to run into Jake again, be certain to use that nickname."

"Call you my queen?"

Her head bobs, sending mussed curls everywhere. "Yes. I always told him I would look good in a crown, and he'd sling mud at me by way of a response."

I howl at her obvious disgruntlement. Setting the ice cream aside, I haul her over my chest before asking bluntly, "How sore are you?"

She scissors her legs back and forth before admitting, "Horseback riding sore."

I groan in agony as my cock twitches.

Her brilliant eyes widen. "What did I say?"

"You mentioned *riding*."

Flinging back the coverlet, Danielle rises from the bed, perfectly comfortable in her skin. "You know what I normally do to ease the soreness?"

Unwilling to miss a moment of being with her, I launch myself from the bed. "What's that?"

"A nice warm bath. That generally takes care of any aches and pains."

Her sleek, wet body sliding all over mine? I clench my fists. Mentally I begin to sing "Row, Row, Row Your Boat." Until Danielle teases me as she enters the bathroom. "And if you want to wash my back, maybe I'll do something about that problem you appear to have."

My control shatters. I stalk into the bathroom to see her bending forward, scooping bath salts into the tub. "Just a few hours ago, you were a virgin!"

She gives me a head-to-toe perusal. "Just because I hadn't taken a man fully inside me doesn't mean I haven't fooled around."

I don't know whether to curse her or kiss her. I'm still debating when she steps forward and slips her hand around my cock. "You shouldn't suffer after you've been so generous, Brendan."

I decide to go with kissing.

CHAPTER TWENTY-FOUR

Danielle

TechMonster1722: "Are you going to CES this year?"

IloveMyMac0101: "I wasn't planning on it. Why?"

TechMonster1722: "I hear StreetPilot is releasing a new version."

IloveMyMac0101: "What? Did they upgrade their electronic maps from the 1950s black and white?"

TechMonster1722: "Hardy har har."

—Online Tech Chat Room

"Phina, where the hell are we supposed to be going?" I twist the paper map around a full three hundred sixty degrees, still uncertain which direction is north.

She mutters an incantation as she leans forward over the steering wheel.

I purse my lips. "As if that's going to help. We're in the middle of nowhere and we're lost."

"We're not in the middle of nowhere, Danielle."

"Sure feels like it."

"No, that's where your family lives. I don't feel like I need bear repellant to visit here."

My stomach pitches as Phina takes another turn at least ten miles over the posted speed limit. Out the window, massive oak trees line the street. Finally, I spy a green and white sign that declares we're about to enter Collyer, Connecticut. "Thank you, sweet baby Jesus. We made it."

"Don't jinx us. We still have to find Main Street," she snaps.

"Why didn't you have Emily bring her new sketches into the city?" I wonder aloud.

"You'll understand when we get there," she replies mysteriously.

Shaking my head as her speed slows to a snail's pace, I can't help but remark, "Are you the same driver who illegally passed someone on a double line not two miles back?"

Her eyes cut to the right. "I have no recollection of that."

"Right," I drawl. "Just like all the other times you almost got us killed on our way to the sticks."

Phina's about to retort, but instead jerks the wheel sharply right and pulls into a parking lot. The building in front of us is magnificent—a Victorian gingerbread mansion with a wraparound porch clearly restored by the touch of a master.

Phina and I make our way up to the front door, the mahogany inset with an enormous stained glass window. *Emily must not do too poorly for herself if she lives here,* is my first thought. "Is this Emily's home?"

"No, this is where the Amaryllis Events office is located."

Despite myself, I'm impressed. Old or not, the building—especially in exclusive Fairfield County, Connecticut—is prime real estate.

Phina reaches for the handle. The catch gives way, and the door swings inward, opening into a grand foyer with flower arrangements that must have cost thousands of dollars perched on pedestals standing sentinel on either side of the staircase. "This is stunning. Someone is taking the right kind of time with this restoration."

"Gorgeous, isn't it?" Phina purrs.

"You've been here before?"

"Just once. For Naomi's wedding dress fitting." Phina tips her chin toward a room to the side of the grand staircase.

That's when I spy Emily lounging in the doorway. Today, she's wearing a sleek blue dress that hugs her figure.

I want one for myself.

Before we can say a word, the door flies open behind us. A slightly Southern-accented voice calls out, "Em, I have your coffee! Ava and Matt said to let you know . . . Oh! I'm so sorry. I didn't realize your appointment arrived." A petite brunette stops short of crashing into me with a tray of drinks. It's hard not to notice the glittery diamonds on her left hand.

That doesn't stop the man on the phone behind her from slamming into her back. He rights her with one hand before she and the coffees topple without a break in his conversation. "Jace, I promise I'll remember to bring you home dinner. Baby, when have I ever forgotten?"

The brilliant aqua eyes of the brunette roll heavenward before she declares to Emily, "More like I'll have to remind him to bring Jace something to eat."

"When isn't that the case, Cass?"

"Hush your mouth, Cassidy. Jason can hear you," the man grumbles.

Stepping around me, the woman—Cassidy—hands Emily her drink and says, "I'd like to offer apologies for our brother, Phillip."

Heels tap as they descend the stairs. My head swings in that direction before the newcomer—an edgy blonde—says drolly, "Why bother, Cass?"

Cassidy frowns. "Because it's the right thing to do, Ali."

"Except if you take that on as your newest responsibility, you'll do nothing else when you're supposed to be running this company."

"Unfortunately, there's a lot of truth in that statement." She shifts the tray to her left hand and offers her hand. "Cassidy Freeman. CEO of Amaryllis Events." Then she shakes Phina's. "Good to see you again, Ms. Hart."

"You as well, Cassidy. I see Phil hasn't changed much."

Emily drawls, "If only, Phina."

Phina chuckles warmly before turning to the other blonde. "I'm sorry, I can't remember which sister of Emily's you are. I've only seen your picture."

The woman in question holds out her hand to Phina. "Alison Freeman."

Emily tips her coffee at the other woman and gives us some context about her family. "Phillip is our oldest sibling, then Cassidy, then me. Alison is next in line."

Cassidy announces proudly, "Ali's also our attorney. She passed the bar in *both* New York and Connecticut on her first try when she was barely twenty-one."

My eyebrows shoot upward. "Wow." The young woman in front of me barely looks old enough to have graduated from law school, not seasoned enough to be a corporate attorney for a company that handles multi-million-dollar weddings—something Phina told me about on the drive from New York.

"Thank you." There's a glimmer in her eyes I recognize from working with Emily. Pride. This family has it in spades.

"She's a—" Cassidy begins.

"Don't you dare say it, Cass," Alison warns.

Cassidy makes the motions to zip her lips and throw away the key. Her aqua eyes darken for a moment with amusement before they blank—frozen, like a porcelain doll. It's as if a ghost swept through her as I watched before she actively shoves it aside.

Emily takes up the banter. "Genius. The word is genius, Alison."

"You did graduate from law school at twenty. Dealing with the legal side of Amaryllis Events is second hand to you by now," Phillip—who is done with his call—proclaims as he joins the conversation.

"Every day, you make it more of a challenge, Phil," Alison grits out.

"Ain't that the truth," Emily mutters as she closes in on Cassidy before taking a sip of her drink.

The two older Freeman sisters have a silent conversation before Cassidy twists, asking, "Where's Mugsy?"

Before anyone can answer, I ask, "Mugsy?"

Emily arches a perfectly groomed brow before admitting, "My dog."

"Is it a he or a she?" I bounce up and down on the balls of my feet in excitement.

Phillip replies, "He. We've—"

The three Freeman women have an enormous coughing fit. Phina grins at their antics.

"*Em's* had him for years."

"Is he a particular breed?"

It's Em who answers simply, "He's a Freeman."

"He's a little bit of everything," Cassidy explains diplomatically.

"And he found his family when he had nothing," Alison murmurs so softly, I know we're not intended to hear.

Phina's head swings back and forth like a pendulum at the sibling's by-play. "Where are your other sisters, Emily?"

"Corinna's setting up a dessert bar for a Daughters of the American Revolution event. Then she's delivering a sweet sixteen cake before that last-minute engagement cake," Cassidy recites.

"And now you appreciate why Cassidy's our CEO," Phillip drawls.

Cassidy narrows her eyes into slits. "She would have been back in time to see Ms. Hart and meet Ms. Madison if you hadn't triple-booked her while I was at the site visit you scheduled for me last week."

Emily and Alison glare at Phillip for committing some cardinal sin.

He holds up his hand. "I don't work our computer systems that well. They were accidents."

"They always are. Somehow, someway, I'll figure out a way to avoid these little mishaps in the future," Cassidy vows.

"Hell, Cass. I was up to my elbows in freesias."

A voice floats down the stairs. "As Ms. Hart might remember, but Ms. Madison certainly wouldn't know, Phil's our florist."

My head and Phina's whip upward. Glorious locks of fire obscure the woman who's been observing us from behind a camera.

Intuitively, I tug my John Deere hat over my face more securely.

"Sorry. That's Holly. She was finishing up in the darkroom," Alison says, a bit of reproach in her voice over my actions.

Before I can fire a remark back, Phina storms to the base of the stairs. "I'm so irritated with you."

A resigned sigh wafts down at her. "Hello, Phina."

"Why didn't you apply for my internship, Holly?" Phina growls.

"Because I need to earn money? Despite having a job I love, I still have school loans to pay off."

Phina's foot stomps on the floor. "We could have worked something out."

As I listen to Phina do battle with the younger woman, the sun glints through the leaded glass windows and highlights a frame.

The image it highlights as if it were beneath a museum spotlight takes my breath away. It could be dismissed as simply a black-and-white print that has zoomed in on the legs of an abandoned playhouse, but the photographer has captured so much more—despair, neglect, and something so fragile.

Hope.

Because at the base of a tangle of weeds, springing up with amazing resiliency, is a perfect lily that to my untrained eye looks like an amaryllis.

I'm pulled toward it. I halt my friend's words by breathing, "Phee." Just her name, but it's enough.

She stops her debate at the wonderment in my voice. Whipping around, she catches sight of what's garnered my attention. Everyone's gone silent as they realize what's captured my interest—incredible untarnished talent. I wonder aloud, "Just how good a baker is your other sister . . .?"

"Corinna," five voices say in unison.

"She's the best there is," Alison says.

"I happen to agree. It's why I don't eat dessert as a rule, but I'll eat anything made by Corinna Freeman," Phina says.

Ruefully, I glance down at my waistline. "It might be a good thing she isn't here."

A titter of laughter accompanies footfalls down the stairs. I whip around in excitement toward Holly Freeman. "This is your photo?"

Holly nods.

"Is this why you named your company Amaryllis Events? Because of this photo?"

The Freeman siblings exchange complicated glances. It's Phillip who explains, "That's actually a tiger lily, Ms. Madison."

"What's the difference?" I ask, genuinely curious.

Phillip makes a sound like I've shot him point blank. All four sisters laugh uproariously. Holly drifts toward the back, clutching her camera to her chest like she wants nothing more than to lift it. I smile at her openly. "It's a stunning photo."

"Thank you." Holly's cheeks flush.

"Now, missy. Where's your updated portfolio? I only saw a few new photos when Emily met Dani." Phina taps her foot impatiently. Cassidy, Phil, and Alison grin at the discomfort on their sister's face.

"Phina . . .," she begins.

"Your talent is ridiculous, Holly," Phina tells her.

"You're just being nice."

"I'm never nice," Phina snaps. "Tell her, Danielle."

I mutter, "Ain't that the truth."

And everyone bursts into friendly laughter.

While they're distracted, Emily moves closer. I say, "Is it always this . . .?"

"Crazy?" Emily supplies helpfully.

"Your word, not mine."

Thoughtfully, Emily's eyes cut over to her family, where her brother now has his arm wrapped around her younger sister. Holly is still clutching her camera like it's an extension of her arm, or maybe her heart, as she holds her own battling with Phina.

Emily studies the scene a minute longer before indicating I should follow her. "No. Normally everyone's more reserved."

What's left unsaid is *toward outsiders*. Her words are more thoughtful instead of hurtful, so I take them as such. I know what it means to hold back. "It must be challenging pleasing others day in and day out. Really, don't feel like you have to do that with me."

Emily quirks a brow. "Maybe in another four or five decades when I've established my brand."

I burst into laughter. "I somehow don't think it will take that long."

"I hope not." Emily pushes a door open. "I understand from Phina you're looking to update your style."

I cast my eyes up to the underbrim of my favorite hat. "I don't imagine you have anything that matches this."

Deadpan, Emily informs me coolly, "The minute I do, they should shut down my studio."

I burst into laughter. When I'm done, I face a rack full of exquisite evening dresses, sexy slips, slinky tops, and varying-length skirts in shades ranging from pale lilac to a shockingly rich violet instead of the more on-trend shocking pink. My heart picks up speed as I approach the rail of outfits, laid out with—"God, there's even a belly chain."

"Like it?"

"Love it. You're a stylist."

"For a very select few."

"Be mine," I plead.

Emily snickers. "Only if you ditch that hat for the red carpet."

"That's a deal so long as you tell me where you found these incredible clothes? Christ"—I pull a skirt off the rack and hold it up—"I think it's actually going to fit."

Emily gives me a mysterious smile before it clicks. "You don't just design wedding gowns, do you?"

Her head shakes. "I can make any piece of clothing you desire."

I drop to my knees and hold the skirt skyward. "Bless you."

Emily grins as I get back to my feet. "There's just one problem."

"What's that?" I ask as I was just about to take a matching inverted *V* strapless top off the rack.

Emily's eyes twinkle. "I forgot to ask Phina if these would be appropriate for any upcoming plans with a certain musician."

I flush hotly. "I feel like I'm already naked."

Emily snarks, "At least he listens to you."

"What makes you say that?" I cock my head to the side.

"He looked gorgeous on the red carpet. Unlike Roger Stephens, who looked atrocious standing next to Sarah Milne." Her lips form a moue of disgust. "Didn't anyone tell them that flaming yellow and brown only remind people of one thing?"

Emily explains it explicitly, which causes me to drop the skirt while I screech with laughter. "For the record, one does not aspire to have their fashion described as baby excrement."

"Stop. I can't breathe." I wipe the tears from my eyes. The designer Phina found me is a firecracker.

When I tell her as much, she winks. "This is why Ali has a dual non-disclosure clause in your contract with Amaryllis."

"Why's that?" I ask, bending over to pick up the skirt.

"So neither of us can ever disclose what comes out of the other's mouth." I catch the wry twist of Emily's lips. "You'd be amazed at what's disclosed in my fitting rooms."

Her eyes flash with anger, sadness, longing, and resignation. I can only imagine if Emily's been dressing the uber elite some of the on-dits she's overheard. "Let me ask you this, Emily. What do you think about my giving my niece a Zac Posen purse for their birthday?"

Her mood at once lifts. "Are you taking applications for new nieces, Ms. Madison?"

"Sorry, no. Especially from women who can't call me by my given name. Let's say it together now. Dani."

"Well, drat. And I really like his new line." Consideringly, she gives me a head to toe perusal. "Make it Em."

"My name? But I've used Dani for a long time."

Her grin is lightning fast and dazzling. I'm amazed by the change it brings to her features. "Nice, Dani. We should make you an honorary Freeman for that kind of comment."

"Thanks, Em. Now, since I'm an honorary family member, how did you all choose the Amaryllis as your logo?"

Emily hands me a skirt and top. "Change into these so I can check the hem. Then I'll tell you the legend instead of forcing you to look it up on our website."

My brows raise beneath my cap. "There's a legend?"

"An incredible one." And Emily starts to educate me on Greek mythology.

CHAPTER TWENTY-FIVE

Brendan

Is Danielle Madison really the right woman for Brendan Blake? More importantly, is he the right man for her?

Maybe they have an open relationship we don't know about. After all, she's cozying up in next to nothing with a gorgeous blond in New York in the picture below while Brendan's still squiring that cute brunette we can't get a snap of.

Let's discuss.

—Nashville Nights

"This is such bullshit! Who the hell are they to make any judgment about Danielle? That's her damn cousin they're speculating about. What the hell must she be feeling?" I shout.

"Calm down, son," Smith says, trying to soothe me.

I glare at him. "You may be dating my mother, but I'm not your son. I'm *nobody's* son. Are we clear?"

Smith bristles. "Completely, *boss*."

I lean forward until I brace my elbows on my knees. "Christ, Smith. I'm sorry. I didn't mean it like that."

He jostles me when he sits down at my side. "I know, kid. I didn't mean to prod the beast at the wrong moment."

I bump his shoulder. "If there's anyone I'll ever be able to point to and say, 'This is my father figure,' it's you."

"Damn. Don't get all mushy now. You've got to get out there and play soon."

I steeple my fingers. "I have feelings for her, Smith. I mean, I really like her."

He shrugs. "What's not to like? She's the most beautiful woman on the planet."

I shake my head. "It's deeper than that. She challenges me on a personal level—like the whole bit about STORM?" Smith nods. "Being a part of something so important is right, but I want to be a better man because of the way she looks at me."

"How does she look at you?"

"Like I'm not made of broken boots," I whisper. The song I penned not long after I took my mother's maiden name was a purging of how small and insignificant I felt in comparison to the megalomaniacal bastard who fathered me. Compared to him, I knew I'd never be more than a pair of worn, dusty, broken boots.

Smith's hand clasps me on the shoulder. "That's how your mother makes me feel."

My lip curls. "Gross."

"Kid, you're thirty-two years old. Do you think your mother wants to read about your exploits in the tabloids?"

I rear back. "What exploits?"

Smith regards me as if I've taken a guitar to the head. "Umm? Your early escapades backstage when you were touring with Small Town Nights?"

I cringe. "Yeah. I wasn't exactly circumspect." God, I even hit on a woman from the stage one night in front of the man she was with when I handed her my hat with my phone number in it.

"For Christ's sake, why do you think your new fan base is in such an uproar? Why do you think hers is? Before they've even had a crack at you, they think you're closin' up shop. Meanwhile, hers thinks you'll cheat on her during every tour stop."

"Fuck. That. And fuck them."

Smith's brow raises just as there's a knock on the door. Kit pops his head around the door. He wiggles his brows up and down before announcing, "A Miss Danielle Madison here for you, boss."

"Smith," I growl in warning.

"On it." The older man leaps to his feet and grabs Kit by the scruff.

Seconds later, Danielle appears in the doorway with a confused expression on her face. "Smith doesn't appear happy."

"He's slightly less enthused than I am."

She quirks her head to the side. "Why's that?"

I fling my arm to the piles of newspapers which berate our friendship, our budding romance. Danielle merely rolls her eyes. "Oh, those."

"That's all you have to say about it?" I'm incredulous.

"Well, it's not as if there's anything to them, Brendan. As you said, there's parts of you that you can't *share* with me. You won't discuss *it*, nor will you apologize for *it*," she emphasizes waspishly.

My control snaps as she throws my own words back in my face. Those words were a final desperate grasp before I knew what it would be like to be enraptured by this woman. Stalking forward, I wait for any sign that she may not want this, want me. Danielle holds her ground, arms akimbo. Her deep violet eyes flash up at me when I hook an arm through hers and yank her against my body. As I lower my head, I growl, "We are so much more than the media could ever dream up in their twisted minds."

"Are we?" she challenges me, her breath merging with mine.

"Damn straight. Just . . ."

"What?"

"Don't hate me later," I say before capturing her lips with mine.

All the noises from backstage disappear as I move my mouth over Danielle's. Our lips settle, tongues tangle. I inhale the soft scent of her perfume. Her taste? God, I've never been addicted to anything but music, and I know she could make me permanently crave her.

I wrap Danielle up in my arms tighter, though I'm not certain how much closer we can get. Her fingers clutching my shirt slide up my chest so she can pull herself flush to my body. Her hands knock my hat off my head, and I growl deep in my throat when she slips her hands through my hair.

I band an arm around her back and sink my fingers into her curls, holding her prisoner.

I never want to let her go.

I drag her backward to find a horizontal surface when a furious pounding interrupts us. Smith shouts, "Five minutes, B!"

Like a bucket of water dumping on me, I spring away from her. Her breathing is labored, cheeks tinged with color. I can't resist pulling her back to brush my lips against hers. She willingly capitulates. Taking soft little nips, I murmur, "Kissing you wasn't what I planned, Danielle."

"What were you planning?"

"To give you a little more time to know what you're feeling, to give us each time to deal with that." I jerk my head behind me to the table of tabloids.

She stiffens in my arms. "Are you seriously telling me you care more about your reputation than me, Brendan?"

I smooth my hand over her hair. "No. What I'm trying to be is careful."

"I'm trying not to be insulted."

"I . . . what?"

"I have never felt the way I do about a man the way I do about you and at the same time never wanted to . . ."

"To what?"

"To strangle him!" Danielle rips herself from my arms and measures my neck with her hands.

I throw my head back and laugh.

She stomps her foot. "It's not funny!"

I haul her back until she's resting fully against me. "Oh, yeah. It really is. If you knew how worried I was about how you would feel about all that garbage . . ."

She holds up a hand. "Wait, you were worried for me?"

I chew my lower lip and nod. Immediately, the fury flees from her magnificent eyes. "Me? You were worried about me?"

This time, I smile and brush a kiss against her lips.

"You're forgiven."

Unannounced, Smith flings open the door. "B, it's . . . oops. Sorry, kids."

With a quick brush of her lips near my ear, she whispers, "I'll be waiting."

Just knowing that makes my blood sizzle. I give her one more lingering kiss before I follow Smith out of the room and through the dark behind the stage.

My fans have no idea the reason they'll get the performance of a lifetime is because of who's waiting for me backstage.

CHAPTER TWENTY-SIX

Danielle

Brendan Blake brought down the house in front of 15,000 fans last night. Backstage, he gave an impromptu interview. When asked what the best night of his night was, all he did was smile intently over our shoulders.

A tall figure sporting a John Deere cap lounged in the shadows.

Maybe there's a third person in his life that's not Danielle Madison or the Nashville brunette?

—New York Entertainment

In the wings, I feel a lick of fire ripple through me as Brendan seduces the crowd with his talent. In between songs, his eyes snag mine for a brief moment as he plays a few chords. He leans into the microphone and rumbles, "Who's hungry for some Blueberry Pie?"

Blueberry Pie? No way.

At the noise of the crowd's intense response, I straighten from where I hide in the shadows.

Brendan leans into the microphone and croons, "***You swore I'd remember this night***." From the hot warehouse to the helicopter flight, to driving around Nantucket, Brendan has memorialized his emotions about our first date.

He prompts the crowd—who's been singing along with every single word—"I need to taste that pie on your lips, but I knew—I knew!— if I did, I'd never get over you. Instead you . . ."

Tears spill down my cheeks as he sings about his surprise gift. His head turns to the side when he sings, "***You mailed a slice of yourself to me***."

I know he can't see me, but I mouth, *I did.* Subconsciously, I did. I mailed a part of myself to Brendan when I sent him the first pie. I wanted him to remember how we felt when we were on the island.

Apparently, he did.

The song ends with Brendan strumming his guitar. "The night that inspired that song was one of the best of my life." Then he leans forward and does something completely unexpected. He murmurs with a private smile, "I want to take us back a few decades. I'd like to call out my friend Amanda Reidel to sing this one with me, if she doesn't mind."

Then there's the infamous keyboard introduction before Brendan strums quickly, along with his keyboard player and Amanda Reidel—the lead singer of Small Town Nights—enters from the opposite side of the stage singing "Dancing Queen."

Brendan's fans go wild, but nowhere as crazy as I do. I'm bouncing up and down like a cheerleader in the shadows. *He did this for me*, is the only thought careening through my mind. I might have sent him a pie, but this? Talk about romantic gestures? This one beats all. *Phina's going to lose her mind when I tell her*, I think as I spin around before boogying down so my rear rests on my heels and then back up.

Smith throws me an amused glance as I sing along to every word of the infamous ABBA song. Brendan is on stage laughing as Amanda catches the tambourine from Brendan's drummer. Soon, they're joined by Amanda's husband Shane—which causes the crowd to go even wilder—and opening act, Morrow O'Brien. They do a quick reprisal of the refrain with all of them on stage.

Then Shane Reidel sings the opening line to "Another Brick in the Wall" while playing the deep throbbing bass line for the crowd.

I'm singing just as loud as anyone in the crowd from the wings. Brendan plays the guitar solo before passing it back to Shane.

And that's when my throat gets dry. I can no longer sing. Because Brendan transitions the legends on stage to another memory that's seared in my mind.

Morrow O'Brien takes the lead singing, singing Jack Wagner's "All I Need." His young voice is a perfect foil for the song about needing more time to be sure of what he feels. But I can't drag my eyes away from Brendan to watch the crowd's reaction. *Does Brendan know I was awake when he sang this to me after the first time we made love?* Tears prick my eyes when I realize that even if he doesn't, Brendan needs to pour out his emotions through music.

I give him my full attention, letting him tell me what he needs to through song.

Brendan sings along with the words even though it isn't his lips at the mic. Through my every movement, every facial expression, I try to show him it's okay—he can have as much time as he needs to be certain about us.

Just as Brendan steps up to the spotlight, he looks directly at me. Then he sings the first line to "Shameless."

My lips part on a gasp. He proceeds to tell every member of his crew, everyone on the stage, everyone in the stadium, that he doesn't have far to fall.

This beautiful lyrical montage tells me more than a simple three words vow ever could. Brendan Blake loves me.

He just told me in his native language.

Brendan continues to serenade me. Amanda supplies the brilliant backup to this epic moment. My hands lift and press against my lips, trying to keep the sobs at bay.

I know no matter what happens in our future, I'll never forget this moment. It's the moment where I realize I'll never stop loving Brendan Blake. Not because he is my storm chaser, but because he brings a joy so bright into my soul simply by being himself, it's impossible not to feel brighter in his presence.

I know it.

His fans know it.

It's time he does.

CHAPTER TWENTY-SEVEN

Brendan

Most of us have unhealthy thoughts and emotions that have either developed as a result of trauma or hardships in their childhood, or the way they were raised. . . .

. . . often times these poisons—and I call them poisons only because they seem to affect our lives in a way that are . . . are very destructive.

—Steven Seagal, Dreams of Tibet—Frontline Interview

Danielle slips from bed after we make love. I grumble, "Can't you lie still, Dancing Queen?"

She laughs softly. "I'll be right back."

"It's"—I roll over and look at my alarm clock—"four o'clock in the morning. What's so important?"

She doesn't say anything. She just gives me a fantastic view as she snatches up my tee from the floor before sliding it over her head. Pressing two fingers against her lips, she aims them in my direction. "I'll be right back," she repeats.

"Hurry," I groan. I twist, propping myself against the headboard and debate the merits of middle of the night sex. Now that I'm awake, I want nothing more than to slide myself into Danielle's slick heat again.

Lacing my fingers behind my head, my lips curve as I think of the way she turned me inside out when we got back to my house a few hours ago. I rotate my shoulder, still feeling the clasp of Danielle's nails digging in after I threw her long legs over my shoulders and feasted until she came.

The first time.

With a smug smirk, I hear her on the stairs and study her as she walks back into the room. Danielle's already remarkable eyes are incandescent. She's carrying a leather-bound planner with her. I roll my eyes. "You left my bed in the middle of the night to . . .?"

"To get my planner."

"Dear God, why?"

"Because you'll be asleep when I leave tomorrow," she huffs.

I flash a smile at her. "True. But who scheduled an early morning flight?"

"If you want, I can change it."

"I want. Change it. Stay for an extra day."

Dani beams at me before reaching for her cell and doing just that. After rearranging her schedule to meld with mine, she plops back onto the bed. She flips open her journal and turns to next week. She faces it at me. Almost every hour except her updated flight time is booked. I let out a long whistle. "Is this telling me you don't want me to take you again?"

She slaps my arm. "No, jackass. I'm trying to figure out when we can see each other next."

I grin. "Give that to me."

She hands it over and cuddles next to my side. I flip through a few pages and my jaw unhinges a bit when I realize the kind of schedule she has coming up. "Photoshoots for Valentino and Chanel, plus you're walking the runway for two shows, and you have work for STORM?" I confirm incredulously.

She waves her hand. "Brendan, I'm more concerned about your schedule. Would you mind writing in your tour dates so I can figure out a way to meet you?"

I lower the book to my lap. "Danielle, when are you going to find time?"

She sits up and her brow furrows. "I'll make time."

My hands lift and fall on the carefully documented pages. "Where? How?"

"For people you love, you make time for them," she declares stubbornly.

Her words hit me with a two-by-four. Danielle Madison—supermodel, internationally recognized face, my blueberry pie Kryptonite—just told me she's in love with me. "Danielle."

Her eyes glow as she rips the planner from my hand. "Look, Brendan, it won't be hard. See? Here I have four days off when—"

"Danielle. Stop," I interrupt her firmly.

She recoils. "What's wrong?"

I feel like I'm going to be ill—so much so, I fling back the covers and head for the en suite. I splash water on my face and in my mouth, trying not to let the panic overwhelm me.

Danielle just waits for me to finish before asking, "What's wrong, Brendan? Tonight at the show, I thought we were on the same page."

"You thought wrong," I whisper. My voice echoes in the tiled space.

She rears back as if I slapped her. "What do you mean?"

"Listen, I'm your first. Don't turn this into too much beyond that."

"So, it's just . . . sex? Is that what you're saying?"

I open my mouth to agree but can't force the words out because I'd be lying if I did. And Danielle abhors liars. Her eyes narrow. "What has you so scared?"

Frantically, I look at the towels, the rugs, the clean shower—something I'd hoped to mess up with her before she left in the morning. Finally, I say, "It's too much for me."

"What is 'too much for you'? Caring? Commitment?"

I gesture weakly between her nude body and mine. "Both?"

"You're a goddamn coward."

I bristle. "Excuse me?"

"You stood up in front of fifteen thousand people tonight and proclaimed you're in love with me, but the moment I say it back, you run for the hills? Well, here's how I feel about that. Fuck you, Brendan."

No, that's not what I did tonight, I think frantically. A little voice inside my head thinks back to my reaction before Danielle ever came backstage. Then the set list. Then how I pleasured her body before I took my own release.

I can't be in love with her. Being in love means being vulnerable and weak, my mind taunts me.

That's when I hear the bedroom door slam.

And I don't care that I'm buck ass naked. I tear off after her, shouting, "Dani!"

She's struggling to shove things into her overnight bag. Her head snaps up at my voice. Tears stain her cheeks. I croak, "No. Not like this."

"Don't worry about me, Brendan. I'm a big girl. I can book a hotel until I get back to New York."

I reach for her and pull her to her full height. Somehow, she's all buttoned up and ready to bail. *How the hell long was I in the bathroom?* I blurt, "It's not you."

A sneer crosses her perfect lips. I squeeze her arms. "It's not a line, Danielle." I think about how to explain when she interjects coolly, "If you would call me a cab, I can be out of your hair in just a few moments."

"No!"

She rubs her hand over her face. "I don't get this. You don't care for me, but you don't want me to leave? What kind of an asshole are you?"

The biggest, I think to myself. I capture one of her hands and haltingly try to give her enough information not to walk out of my life. At least, not yet. "My mom, she had a difficult time with my . . ."

"Father?" Danielle supplies the word.

"I don't use that word when it pertains to him. He's a douchebag of the highest order."

"What does he have to do with us?"

"Everything."

"That makes no sense."

"That man made my mother's life a living hell. He cheated on her for as many years as I can remember. He never cared for her or—"

Her fingers squeeze mine. "You?"

"Exactly. I know I'll never be able to go the route of traditional love and commitment because of the influence he imparted on me. I don't know how to love. I can never imagine myself married. As for children? No. Never."

She studies my face for long moments. Finally she sighs and I let out a breath I didn't know I'd been holding when she capitulates, "Okay."

What? "What does that mean?"

Her next words slice through me. "Since no one has taught this to you, let me. Love isn't meant to trap a person, it's meant to free them, lessen the burden. I never want you to think my feelings for you are selfish. Even if you were to . . . feel things for me and couldn't take a step to commit to me, because that's all that your . . . emotions . . . could give, I'll accept that."

"You will?" I choke out.

"But don't ever lie to me, Brendan. If you don't . . . care about me anymore, let me go. I deserve better."

"You deserve everything, but I can't stand the idea of you walking out that door." Gently, as if I'm terrified she's going to lunge for the knob the minute I loosen my hold, I pull her against my body.

Her breath huffs out before her arms wrap around me. "I won't leave you, Brendan."

"Promise?"

"I promise."

For long moments we stand in my foyer, and I say a million prayers of thanks for the woman in my arms. Because no matter where I go on this planet, she's going to live inside me.

An insidious thought worms its way in. *Is this what love feels like?*

I press a kiss to the crown of her head and think, *Maybe. But now I have time to figure it out.*

"Let's get some sleep. Then I'll cook you breakfast in the morning."

Danielle snorts. "That will be a first."

I want to tell her the first of many, but I can't push the words past the watermelon in my throat. And I know what's causing it.

Fear. Fear of my whole world imploding.

PERFECTLY FREE

CHAPTER TWENTY-EIGHT

Brendan

Danielle Madison was spotted striding through LaGuardia Airport this evening.

Neither the blond god nor Brendan Blake were at her side.

Does this mean she's done with both men?

—New York Entertainment

"This place says so much about you," Danielle declares after we've finally crawled out of bed after our midnight altercation. We're sitting on my back deck having what might pass for brunch the next afternoon.

Still reeling from the fact this glorious woman stayed when she had every reason to slam out the door, I'm distracted as I watch her hoover a plate of bacon and eggs. "Hmm?"

She pauses eating and waves her fork in the air. Her blond curls are askew and, dressed in only a dark shirt she snagged from my closet, her eyes appear a deeper purple than usual. "It's private,"

"And that's a bad thing?"

"Not at all."

Curious, I ask, "What else does my home say about me?"

Without hesitating, Danielle says, "It's screams settled, roots, with a healthy dose of taste."

My lips curve into a grin before admitting, "That's because my mama couldn't wait to help me decorate when I moved in."

Danielle stretches out her long legs. "I promise I won't tell a soul."

"I'm obliged." My words come out tinged with humor.

"She has excellent taste. Your home is welcoming and comfortable. I have to give her props—she's right."

"About what?"

"That hint of pine-fresh scent fits right in."

"Let me guess, you'd prefer it more if it was lemon."

She hums. "Now that you mention it . . ."

I brace, waiting for her words.

"No." She inhales deeply. "Pine is perfect for here. It's like the scent accentuates what your house is saying."

"Which is?"

"It's calling out to the wind, harnessing the wild. Completely you." Dani lifts her arms to encompass my house and the surrounding trees. While I'm still reeling from her armchair analysis, she asks a very simple question. "Why should it feel like someone else?"

"Everyone wants to change something about me."

"God, I hope you don't let them. You wouldn't be the man you are if you did."

If you dropped a ton of bricks on my chest, I'd be less surprised at her words. "You really don't want to change anything?" *Especially about me?*

"No. Wait. That's a lie. There are three things I'd recommend."

I steady myself. "Go ahead."

"You should move that kickass bowl on your kitchen counter into the sunroom. The glass is exquisite, and I'm dying to know where you got it."

Flabbergasted, I say, "It was a housewarming gift from my mama."

"Again, her taste is exceptional." She points between two trees and says, "Since you're lucky enough to have a backyard, you should totally invest in a hammock. I have a very clear image of you chilling when you're home, strumming away on your guitar."

"And the third?"

"If you haven't met already, let me introduce you to Bar Keepers Friend to clean your counter grout. That stuff works miracles."

I hold up a hand. "That's it? That's what you would change?"

"Nothing else jumps out at me. Oh, wait. Don't break my heart with your next answer."

The expression on her face is so intense, internally, I brace. "What is it?"

"Tell me you put up a whopper of a Christmas tree."

"I do." Deflecting her line of questioning, I turn the tables. "Do you?"

Talking about Christmas might lead to a discussion about the kids, and I'm nowhere near ready for that. Besides, I want to know more about this woman who is invading my life without trying.

She nods. "Every year, Dad and Uncle Jeremy drag the three of us—me, Jake, and my niece Jenna—into the woods behind their houses in upstate New York. There's a Christmas tree farm there."

"And the owners let them cut one down?"

"Two. Once for each house. That's in exchange for our parents allowing farm vehicles to cut through their yard throughout the course of the year."

"Seems like a fair trade."

"It's worked out well." Danielle's quiet as she contemplates her next words. "It was at our town's Christmas tree festival that my first agent spotted me."

"How old were you?"

"Sixteen. Mom yelled for the cops and attempted to have Ford Coughlin arrested for soliciting."

I'd just lifted my coffee to my mouth and somehow manage to spit it back in the mug. "Ford Coughlin? The Ford Coughlin? Once married to your friend Phina Hart, Ford Coughlin?"

"One and the same. In my opinion, it was the least he deserved."

"The man launched your career. How can you say that?"

When her face turns toward mine, I find the same wariness she wore the night we met. I suck in a breath and brace for her next words. "Because Ford actually did proposition me that night. He might have thought I was legal, but it was a blatant proposition, nonetheless."

"Excuse me?" My voice is low and lethal.

Danielle's lips curve faintly. "Why are you so shocked, Brendan? It's not the first time it happened, nor will it be the last."

"Because . . ." I can't form words through my fury.

"Fortunately for Ford, someone else who saw my face that day honored his lies. It saved his bacon—then. She later crucified him in their divorce."

"Phina?"

"You've met her. Can't you picture her exacting her revenge?"

"Easily."

"Phina was more intimidating than Ford."

"I bet she was." I sip my coffee, trying to lower my heart rate.

Dani continues, "She walked up and agreed with everything Ford said and then offered to shoot my portfolio."

"What an auspicious start to an incredible career."

Danielle pulls her legs up beneath my shirt before wrapping her arms around them. "That night . . . after we"—she points between me and her —"met, I was seriously contemplating giving it all up. Just walking away. Phina convinced me we had more to do and the stage to make a difference. STORM gives me a purpose."

"Why did you call it that? Does it stand for anything?"

Her head twists away and she stares out over the landscape. "We named the charity STORM simply because not everyone charges headfirst into a potentially violent situation. It's called the bystander effect or bystander apathy. It isn't intentional, but human nature causes people to freeze—caught up in their own fears. They question whether they should help? What will happen to them?"

"It seems wrong."

"It's self-protection," she counters. Then she purses her lips. "Have you ever stood in the middle of a storm?

"I can't say I have."

Dani lifts her face to the sun and whispers, "Storms are unstoppable. They're coming regardless of if you want them to or not. And when they hit, look out."

Her words slam into me. "I'm your storm."

"Brendan, you're a complete weather system." Her grin wry when she admits, "Half the time, you're a tornado. You step into a room and steal my breath away."

I tug her hand and yank her from her chair and onto my lap. "Let's see if I can manage that in a different way."

By the time my lips meet hers, my head's spinning as well.

It is long moments later before I have a rational thought. When I pull my lips back, I wonder, *If I'm Danielle's storm, how do I classify what she makes me feel?*

Then she's tugging my head forward again, and I forget trying to figure it out.

CHAPTER TWENTY-NINE

Danielle

Brendan Blake was sporting one hell of a smile on stage in Atlanta tonight. He was seen flirting from the edge of the stage with fans.

It's no surprise the handsome country star is pulling in women to his show in droves. The real question is what's happening backstage?

—Nashville Nights

"Maybe it was all too much for him to take?"

I lay on my bed in my condo, staring at the shadows dancing around the ceiling. There's an overwhelming pain in my heart as I replay the events of Nashville in my mind.

"I'd have sworn he was telling me he loved me," I whisper aloud to the empty room. I force myself to go over everything from the moment I first saw him that night.

His demonstrativeness.

His declarative gestures.

His possessiveness.

Do I regret sharing what I did with him?

I roll to my side and stare out the window before answering myself. "No, I don't regret telling him I love him. Love isn't a mistake."

But what if it costs me Brendan?

"Then the world keeps spinning round and round. Because if he can't love me, then his heart was never meant for mine," I conclude sadly.

I pick apart the reasons he gave me for not wanting to love. Then I jackknife on my mattress in horror. "Is Brendan feeling what Jake does? Was the betrayal to his mother so severe he won't trust what's in his heart?" Does it mean shutting mine out?

Will I love him any less?

I flip back, already knowing the answer.

"I can feel your heart calling out to mine even when you're not nearby. It isn't the proximity. Now, if only you could love me in return, that might yank me from this agony." Admitting that, I close my eyes in an attempt to escape the pain of loving but not being loved in return.

Not for more than my body.

"I don't know what to think, Phee," I confide over coffee a few days later. I'm still waiting for Brendan to call me since we kissed goodbye on his doorstep in Nashville. "Maybe it was all too much for him to handle."

"After what you told me? You want the truth."

"Always."

"Find someone with a backbone. There's a lot more that happens in a relationship that's going to cause a rift. You need a man who will be at your side during your darkest days."

"What about him? Am I not supposed to be there for his?"

Her head swerves to the side, unable to cede my point.

"Should I just walk because he has something he isn't ready to share yet?"

"I hate when you're right, darling." She leans forward and presses her hand into mine. "I just hate the sorrow marring your beautiful face."

"It's just a face," I mutter.

"And it's a reflection of the heart beneath. What do you want to do?"

"In a perfect world?"

"In any world."

"I'd call Brendan and talk. Just . . . talk. Try to figure out why he's suddenly gone cold on me." I lean forward and rest my forehead in my hands. "Christ, Phee. I told him I didn't expect his love in return. What is he trying to do to me?"

Her hand hesitates before she smooths it over my back. "Perhaps he's doing what he thinks is best if he doesn't feel the same way."

My shoulders heave as the first sob rips from me. "I hate liars."

"Him?"

I catch my breath and wipe my nose on the napkin Phina hands me. "Myself. I said I would accept whatever he felt for me." I lift my tear-stained face to my best friend. "I'm so full of shit. All I want is for him to love me."

She slides from her chair to join me on the couch and wraps me in her arms. "That is the only thing any of us want in life, Dani. Now, give me your pain. Share it with me."

I give into the storm Brendan created. I can't stop the surge of cries and tears that come from the depth of my soul.

CHAPTER THIRTY

Brendan

TechMonster1722: Rumor has it West Moore bought 2,000 acres of land just outside of London

IloveMyMac0101: Dear God. Why?

TechMonster1722: Apparently, he's going to build the headquarters of Moore Software Worldwide.

IloveMyMac0101: Best of luck to our friends
on the other side of the pond. They can
keep him.

—**Online Tech Chat Room**

"What do you want?" I snap.

"To establish the welfare of my children," comes the upper-crust British accent that never fails to spike my anger.

"My"—I emphasize the word—"brother and sister are well."

"Put them on the phone."

I clench my teeth knowing this man stands between me having time with Sula and Joshua before they legally can make their own decisions. *Just a few more years*, I remind myself. Then I can forget West Moore even exists. Tamping down my initial reaction, which is to hang up, I inform him, "They're outside playing soccer—"

"Football."

I take a moment before responding with what I want to, which is something along the lines of "when you actually begin to parent them, then you can call their activities whatever the hell you want."

"Then I'm going to give them each a driving lesson before we have dinner with a few people." I don't bother to mention one of those people is my mother. I suspect the misogynistic bastard already knows.

"Why bother teaching them on your American vehicles when they will just need to learn again on European models? Bloody waste of time."

Of course, he fixated on what I'm doing wrong instead of the happiness of his children. My lips twist, but not with any pleasure. "Ah, but it's my time."

"And their minds are wasting away, Brendan."

"They don't appear to mind."

"A problem I'll rectify when they return home, if I must."

I mimic his clipped, aristocratic tone. " 'If I must.' Christ, West, they're your children, not a science experiment. How about letting them enjoy themselves?"

"Don't think I haven't tried that."

"Really?"

That's when he rips a dagger through the fragile stitches of my heart—a heart Danielle's been piecing back together. "I let Glenda rear you, and look how well that turned out. A country musician after all the schooling I financed? Ludicrous."

The fire pumping through my blood freezes when ice fills my veins at the slur he cast against my mother. "Don't. Don't you say a word about my mother, you philandering piece of . . ."

"Brendan?" I hear JB call from the other room. "Can we finish the tea?"

I inhale sharply to regain my composure before answering back, "Sure. Leave the pitcher in the sink."

"Will do!" comes his cheerful response.

Thousands of miles away, West is silent. Before I can draw first blood, he stutters, "I never . . . Pass along my regards to your mother."

"And your children?" I challenge.

"You apparently understand them better than I do. Do as you will. However, I expect them back before Joshua is due to return to boarding school." Before I can revive a different longstanding argument between us—that he allow his children to remain living with me—he swiftly disconnects the call.

After throwing the portable on the desk, I lean back in my chair and replay the call in my mind before concluding, "Asshole."

Just as I do, my mother breezes into my office without a care. Interpreting my mood correctly, she asks, "And by your tone, I presume your father is well?"

My lip curls. She chuckles before coming around my desk and hitching her hip on it. "Sweetheart, you grew into a fine man."

"Not according to him."

"And you care, why?" Her words shake me to the core. She leans over and cups my chin, exactly the same way she did when she explained why she was taking back her maiden name of Blake.

It means what she's about to say is life-altering.

"Brendan, you are not your father."

"I'm not?" Quickly I catch her up on what happened on my last night with Danielle—how I shattered her illusion I was a man built for happily ever afters. "What right do I have to dump a ready-made family in her lap?"

"Brendan, the fact you're even asking these questions proves how different you are from your father.

"All I've done is evade her questions and lie by omission. And all she's asked for is honesty."

My mother doesn't say a word. Instead, she chews her lip. "Elaborate."

"I sidestep questions about family. She's visits me here, and I scramble for days to remove all traces of the kids for fear of her stumbling over something that will prompt an inquisition. I'm not living my life. I'm trapped in a dual one."

"Do you want to tell her about Sula and Joshua?" Mom probes gently. What she's really asking is, are things serious enough with Danielle to let her into this part of my life.

"Without question." I lean forward and brace my elbows on my knees. She runs her fingers through my hair. "Danielle has the largest heart of anyone I've ever met."

"Then let her in, all the way in."

I lift exhausted eyes to meet hers. "Mom, it's different now."

"Because of who you're becoming? Who she is?"

"Partially, yes. But think of the kids. What would it do to them if it came out and the paparazzi swarmed outside West's home because the tabloids broke the story about their country singer brother? West would never let them see me again and we both know it."

Her fingers still, a sign she's heard me.

"I can't risk their happiness, and I sure as hell won't hold Danielle's hostage." I flop backward.

"So what are you going to do?"

I wince. "It's more like what I did. I told Danielle I'm not interested in marriage, kids. If she wants to be with me, it's without those commitments. That's how it's going to be between us."

My mother nods. I begin to relax until she calmly states, "You have more of your father's stupidity in you than I thought."

My head whips to the side as if she actually slapped me instead of verbally filleting me. "Excuse me?"

"Your father never understood this life lesson either." She leans down until her pale eyes bore into mine. "There is no perfect time to fall in love. Nor is love perfect. It's flawed from the start. After all, beings with the capacity for love are flawed. That doesn't mean it shouldn't be treasured. Throwing it away in search of perfection is a travesty."

For the first time, I truly appreciate the damage my father inflicted upon my mother with his lies and perpetual affairs. Quietly, I ask, "Did you love him?"

"Every moment I was with him and for a long time after," she replies honestly.

"Do you love Smith the same way?"

"No."

"That's it? I don't get any more?"

Her smile lights up an already beautiful face. "With Smith, I found the place my heart is safe to land." Her simple words undo me.

"God, Mom. That's what I feel when I'm with Danielle."

"Then don't throw love away. I know you, Brendan. The man you are is free of the demons that live inside your father. Despite your fears, you're free to live, free to love."

"That's the problem."

"What is?"

"I don't think I am." And with that, I describe the agreement West makes his children abide by. I endure her fury when she realizes what a true bastard my father is. I then explain the pact between Sula, Joshua and me to not let anyone know the truth of our relationship unless we all agree. "Now you see how I lie to Danielle every moment we're together. How can I ask her to commit to a man who doesn't control his own destiny?"

For once, there's no motherly advice. Just silence. Bitterness sweeps through me. "Yeah. That's what I thought."

CHAPTER THIRTY-ONE

Danielle

Supermodel Danielle Madison showed exactly what New Yorkers are made of when she hurled a glass of champagne into software king West Moore's face at the Plymouth party tonight.

Good for you, Dani. I hope someone handed you another one to drink straightaway.

—New York Entertainment

With my back to the party, I ask Phina, "I have a gross feeling."

Immediately her eyes drop to my glass. "Do you think someone spiked the champagne?"

"Not that kind of sick. I'm fairly certain I was just propositioned."

"Here?" Phina's voice holds a wealth of shock. The soiree we're attending is a fundraiser for STORM.

I nod definitively.

Her lip curls. "Who was it?"

"That's just it. I don't know him, yet I feel like I should. Something about him is familiar, but I can't quite place him."

Phina's eyes dart around the room. "Describe him."

"Mahogany hair, liberal gray. Custom tux. Diamond studs. Unusual eyes."

Phina stills. "Unusual as in a gemstone green?"

"Snap. That's it. Who is he?" I rub my hands up and down my bare arms to ward away the feeling of the man's fingers dancing over my skin.

Skin Brendan spent hours kissing just weeks before.

Phina's amused. "He's big money."

"Money doesn't buy class."

She mutters, "West Moore thinks it does."

I frown. "I know that name."

"Chairman and CEO of Moore Software Worldwide. One of the richest people on the planet. Not bad to look at and if you were looking for a sugar daddy, I'd say you struck microchips. That being said, rumor has it he treats women abominably."

"Charming."

Phina's face is angelic when she asks, "Not interested in the lure the esteemed Mr. Moore is casting?"

I hold up the hand not clutching my champagne glass. "First, I have more self-respect. Second, he's got to be older than my father."

Phina nods, eyes dancing.

"Third, I have a reputation I worked hard for. Fourth, I have my own money. And finally"—I'm on the verge of yelling at this point, uncaring if anyone overhears—"I'm in love with Brendan!"

That's when I hear the clipped British accent that propositioned me earlier from directly behind me. "Brendan? As in Blake?"

In a fury, I whirl around and confront the megalomaniac. His eyes travel over my body again as I snap, "What's it to you?"

"He has exceptional taste. I should give the boy more credit."

Before I can stop myself, I hurl the contents of my champagne glass into West Moore's face. "Go to hell."

Much to my surprise, he simply reaches into his pocket for a handkerchief and mops the dripping mess off his face. "I have a permanent residence there already, Ms. Madison."

After that odd little comment, he spins on his heel. My eyes narrow as I stare after him, wishing he would leave. Instead, he stops a server for a drink.

I feel West Moore tracking my every move, ruining what was supposed to be a glamorous night out with Phina. "Can we go?"

Phina agrees readily. "Yes. I'm finding it a tad disturbing how fixated he is on you."

"You're not the only one," I mutter.

We quickly gather our wraps, make excuses to our hosts, and leave.

The next morning, I'm woken way too early by my bedside phone ringing. Groggily, I reach for it. "Hello?"

"Things are not always as they appear, Ms. Madison. A lesson I hope you will appreciate as you learn the truth."

I'm left shaken, not because the caller disconnected after imparting such an ominous message, but because the person who delivered it used the same clipped tone West Moore did the few moments we spoke at the party.

CHAPTER THIRTY-TWO

Brendan

Country music officially has a new number one on both the country and pop charts. Brendan Blake, who first hit the scene with his song, "Broken Boots," has topped US charts with his new summer hit, "Blueberry Pie."

With a career that has nowhere to go but up, one wonders who he'll be taking with him to this year's CMAs. Will it be the mystery brunette he's been dating or the face the world recognizes, Danielle Madison?

Either way, there's nothing that can stop this singer from dominating awards season.

—Nashville Nights

I'm desperate for a moment where the specters of my past stop hovering over my shoulder, ready to destroy the small slice of happiness I've managed to carve out for myself.

What would it be like if the world found out after all these years? I wonder briefly. Then I recall the implications of what it would do to my relationship with Joshua and Sula and quickly tamp down my wayward dreams.

As I listen to the real estate agent drone on and on about the acreage and her breathless remark of "the remarkable size is extraordinary," I feel absolutely nothing. Nothing other than wanting Danielle here, by my side, helping me make this decision. "If I haven't screwed everything to hell," I curse.

"Excuse me?" The agent places her hand on my arm.

An offer. One I quickly shrug off. She steps back and immediately taps into her professionalism. "I'm not certain you'll find another piece of property of this size meeting your unique specifications, Mr. Blake."

I give the land an assessing gaze. From where I'm standing, it's nothing but forest, but the aerial photos and description make it ideal for what I want for my future.

Our future—mine, the kids, and Danielle's.

That is, if I don't manage to completely fuck things up. I quickly make up my mind about both the land and my course of action. "Put in an offer." I low ball the amount on the listing.

She frowns. "They won't like it."

"That's less the amount it's going to take to clear a road into this place for construction. They should expect that kind of negotiation."

Spinning on my heel, I stalk back to my truck. The agent calls out, "Wait! Mr. Blake! Don't you want to see the other parcels of land?"

I stop short and call over my shoulder, "I know what I want."

And I do. I want it all—singing, the kids, and Danielle.

The only question remaining is, can I have it?

I hop into the truck and head back toward town. "Guess there's only one way to find out."

Sula and Joshua watch me somberly as I explain everything about my relationship with the woman they only know as the supermodel, Danielle Madison. "She's so much more than that to me."

"Is she really as pretty as she looks in photos?" Joshua wonders.

"To be honest, she's more beautiful," I tell him.

"I want to be you someday, B," he declares.

I frown and inform him, "I don't love her because of what she looks like."

"Why do you love her, B?" Leave it to Sula to ask the impossible and expecting an answer.

My head drops as I try to put into words the certainty of emotions coursing through me. I swallow convulsively while trying to describe to my baby sister the depth of feelings I have for Danielle that have been tying me into a knot. Hoping she and Joshua understand, I say, "Loving Danielle makes me feel free. I can't go back to feeling trapped within my own body. And that's what it would be if I don't have her in my life."

I shouldn't have worried. My siblings may be over sixteen years younger than me, but they, too, are children of West Moore. Their education wasn't protected and insular. It was a curriculum of hard knocks and emotional blows. Sula relaxes. "Then I vote yes. We bring in Danielle—you said people call her Dani, right?"

"People close to her do. I like to be different."

"I vote we bring Dani into the family? Joshua?"

"I really wish you'd stop calling me that blasted name," he grumbles.

"And what exactly would you like me to call you? Or do I get to choose? You've been saying you don't want to be Joshua all summer. Who do you want to be?" Sula asks sweetly.

His eyes lift to mine and hold. "You call Brendan, 'B.' "

"That's because we agreed it was safer," I say.

"I want to grow up to be just like you," Joshua whispers desperately. His simple words shatter my heart in two.

"Joshua," I manage through a throat that's closing rapidly.

But it's Sula who solves this problem like she does so many others. "So, go by your initials. Joshua Basset Moore. JB"—her eyes, those exquisite emeralds, fasten on mine as I lift my head and meet her gaze—"and our B."

Then she convinces Joshua, JB—Christ, this will be like the football thing—into siding with her with an inner surety I'll never quite understand. Sula makes the decision fait accompli by announcing, "And see? The timing is wonderful. B can introduce you to his Dani as JB, yes?"

And without hesitation, JB agrees, "Yes."

I sag in relief before every muscle in my body locks up. "Now, I just have to tell Danielle."

One ring.

Two.

"Come on. Pick up," I beg.

Three.

Four.

Finally, "Brendan?" She sounds out of breath.

"Is everything okay?" I ask anxiously.

"I was . . . it doesn't matter. I haven't heard from you." Her voice flattens.

Not accusing. Not angry. Just accepting.

Defeated.

I rush the words out. "I need to see you. Is there any way for you to make it to the show in Nashville this week? Maybe come back to my house with me? We really need to talk."

Her voice is remote when she repeats, "You want me to come home with you."

"I know. It sounds wrong, but it's the only place I can think of where we can talk privately. I was a complete jackass." The reason why is one of the many things I need to share with Danielle.

As open and honest as she always is, Danielle says, "I don't know that I can put myself through this again so soon, Brendan."

"I've been thinking—"

She keeps talking. "We obviously aren't on the same page."

"Danielle, I'm in love with you." There's an eerie silence on the other end of the line. I don't know if she's in shock, but I take the silence to mean she's actually listening. "I love you. I have a number of things I need to explain, but the fact that you doubted that I love you is not something I can live another minute with you questioning."

"Then . . ." Her voice is hesitant.

"Then, what?"

"There's no one else?" Before I can reply, she rushes out with, "When we were together, talking regularly, I ignored the paparazzi, Brendan. Since we last spoke, it's been difficult to do that."

I close my eyes in pain as I recall some nasty innuendos printed in the last few days. "I imagine it has been." My need to keep my personal life just that has always been a battle with my protective instincts toward my family. Now that Danielle's a part of it, that emotion is at a full-out war. "Come to me. Please. I'll explain everything."

She sucks in a breath before asking only one question. "When?"

"Can you be here tomorrow?" I pray the answer is yes, because on what will be one of the worst days of any year—the day Sula and Joshua return to England—I need Danielle in my arms. I need to lay out the complications of my life before determining if she can live with the secrets and lies of omission, despite her insistence of truth. I need to plead with her to forgive me for being a stubborn ass about love when it's entirely possible I fell in love with her over blueberry and lemon pie.

"I'll be there. Tell me where," she reiterates.

After I give her the information she needs, we disconnect. That's when I realize she never pushed for an answer from me about whether there was someone else in my life. *Maybe she doesn't want to know, or maybe she intuitively suspects. But there's no way she'll ever believe there are two people involved.*

No one would. That's how good we've all become at our little subterfuge.

CHAPTER THIRTY-THREE

Danielle

"I have no desire to suffer twice, in reality and then in retrospect."

—Sophocles, Oedipus Rex

"Thanks for meeting me at the side door, Carson," I mumble, embarrassed. "I hate to take you from your warm up. I don't know where Brendan or Smith are."

"Happy to do so . . . Holy crap!" Carson shouts. He squeezes my arm. "Stay right here, Dani."

I feel every ounce of blood leech from my head at the sight of the light that's trapped a young man's leg. What's worse is that it's bent at an angle it really shouldn't be. "Is that a bone?"

Carson reaches over to the table I'm standing near and snatches up a walkie-talkie. "We need an EMT. Door three. Do you copy?"

A voice comes through, "I copy. Injuries?"

"I have no fucking idea. It's a member of the crew. This is Carson—Blake's drummer."

"Clear the line. We need to keep it open."

"Just get here now."

My stomach churns. "I-I have to . . . need some air."

He points me to a door and takes off at a dead run, shouting, "Where the fuck is Smith? Someone find him and Brendan, ASAP!"

I stumble outside and try to subdue my nausea by breathing through my mouth. I pray deeply for the unknown member of the crew when I spot Smith exiting one of the buses. I race up to him before the door shuts behind him. "Smith! Smith!"

His eyes grow wide before he grips my arms with both hands. "What are you doing out here without an escort?"

I fling the stack of plastic cards around my neck over my shoulder before I get in his face. "That is the least of your concerns."

He studies me before the anxiety wipes from his face, leaving nothing but business behind. "What do you mean, Dani?"

"One of the big light things." I gesture upward.

His face takes on an ashen cast. "A lantern. What about it?"

"It landed on the leg of one of . . ." Smith doesn't wait for me to finish my sentence. He abruptly drops my arms and sprints for the same door I stumbled through.

Feeling better now that Smith's been notified, I lean against the side of the bus. I welcome the gust of cool air that washes over my skin. Unfortunately, it also flings open the door next to me. Head shaking, I murmur, "Smith, you need to make sure the door latches behind you," as I move to close the door.

And then I freeze.

Because I hear Brendan's voice, clear as day. "It's already in the works. Sula, Joshua—"

"JB," the two voices correct him in unison.

He sighs with patience. "JB. You both have to promise to behave yourselves."

That's when I hear a giggle from a young girl, quickly followed by a choked laugh from a young man.

He speaks first. His voice is accented, demanding, "When will we get to see you again?"

"Soon, buddy."

Then a coltish warble as she issues her own order. "You promise?"

"I promise, princess. Every time you're not by my side, I'm incomplete. You both know how much I love you." Brendan's voice is rife with love and commitment—one which I knew from his own lips I would never have from him.

And now I know why.

Which one of the other women is the mother of his children, I think painfully. Rightfully so, his children are his priority, but why did he have to lie to me? That was the only thing I asked of him: not to lie. Every other choice was mine to make, mine to come to grips with—including falling in love with him. I quietly latch the door to the bus before scanning to the left, then to the right.

Tossing my hair over my shoulder, I walk to the security guard working the gate and ask, "How do I get out of this place?"

His eyes bug out when he recognizes my face. "Um, ma'am?"

"This is an exit, correct?" I turn my face and swipe at my tears.

He leans over and hisses, "Ms. Madison, beyond that gate are about a hundred reporters who heard Carson report an injury over the walkie-talkie. If you're trying to leave, hide your face, use your orange badge, and disappear through the door over there." He jerks his chin over my shoulder.

I lift deadened eyes to his before mouthing, *Thank you.* Stumbling away, I reach into my purse for my John Deere cap. The slogan of the company my father works for comes to mind—Nothing runs like a Deere. *Well, tonight, nothing runs like a Madison,* I think before I tuck my hair beneath it. Sliding on a pair of sunglasses, I use my orange badge and slip through the doors.

Unnoticed.

I leave the stadium with minimal fanfare and snag a cab just as a bunch of drunk college students tumble out of it. I inform the driver, "I need to pick up my bags before I go to the airport."

"It's your dime, lady. Where to first?"

I give him Brendan's address. Fifteen minutes later, I leap out of the car. "I'll be right back."

His drawled, "Meter's runnin'. Don't bother me any," reassures me he won't leave without me.

I dash up the stairs and see my bag, waiting at the foot of the stairs. *Get it and go, Danielle,* I advise myself.

But I can't.

Brendan led me through the kitchen the last time I was here when we entered the house from the garage. I know he'll come through this room when he comes in tonight—*presuming he's not with his kids,* I think bitterly.

My head swivels from left to right. I find what I'm looking for in the built-in writing nook—a scratch pad and a pen. Heart pounding, I put pen to paper.

Dear Brendan,

There are feelings inside me that don't have a name yet.

Since they're singularly unpleasant, it's not fair for me to be around you while I sort through them as you're going through your own struggles at the moment.

You see, I lied too. I don't just want your here and now, I want your forever. And tonight, I realized that's impossible. You say you love me, but that love is for now, when apparently there's something more permanent lodged in your heart.

I know . . .

I need some time to come to grips with everything before I face you, including the fact that had you been honest, I would have loved them too.

I'll be in touch.

Still in love with you,

Danielle

I read the note over and over. It isn't until the taxi driver sounds his horn that I fling the pad and pen on the counter. I grab my weekender and lock up Brendan's house.

Making my way down the front steps, the cab driver slides from his seat to help me with my bag. "Lady, I hope you have cash for this," he mumbles as he tosses my bag into the trunk.

I slide into the back and stare at the house I was certain, in my heart, could have become a home had the man inside just let me in. "Money is the least of my worries. Please take me to the airport."

He doesn't say a word, just begins navigating Brendan's long driveway.

CHAPTER THIRTY-FOUR

Danielle

Danielle Madison boarded a helicopter for Nantucket at Teterboro Airport. It's late in the season for the supermodel to be heading to her beach retreat when she's supposed to be flying to Paris soon for Fashion Week.

—New York Entertainment

"I'll be fine, Mom. A little time alone on the island will do me some good."

My mother isn't buying what I'm selling. "Phina called. She spilled the beans. What you need is a cast-iron skillet to whale that man upside the head with."

I can't argue with her. "Mom, can we leave it for now? I just need . . ." What? Time? Will any amount of time clear the insidious thoughts from my mind? I try to put what's filling my head into words. "It isn't that he . . . it would have been before . . . it's just . . ."

My mother gets to the heart of the matter with two simple words. "He lied."

"Yes."

"And after everything you saw Jake go through with Michelle, you can't handle being in love with a liar."

My head drops against the cool glass. I stare sightlessly out the doors at the view I paid a small fortune for. *Maybe that's because I've come here every time life's fallen to pieces.* I told Brendan that during our first date.

I knew there would be no way I could stay at Brendan's house and be able to look him in the eye, let alone share a bed with him. That would be impossible since I'd confront him the minute he walked through the door—and he'd be unable to deny the truth any longer.

The tabloids were right about the other women in his life. The question is, how right were they? Was he with them when he was with me?

I whisper, "He has children."

"How old are they?"

"Maybe Jenna's age or a bit older? There are two—a boy and a girl."

"Where have they been all this time?" She asks so shrilly I'm not certain the screen on my new iPhone can sustain the sound without cracking.

"I don't know," I reply flatly.

An uncomfortable moment of silence extends between us. Then she whispers, "Tell me how you found out."

I lean my body fully against the jamb, no longer seeing the crashing ocean waves. Instead, I'm transported back to the moment Smith raced away from Brendan's tour bus to help the injured crew member without warning. And heard the adolescent giggle from the girl.

And the broken laugh from the young man.

Then their voices. First, the accented voice demanding, *"When will we get to see you again?"*

"Soon, buddy."

A delicate voice with an indistinctive warble as she issued her own order, *"You promise?"*

"I promise, princess. Every time you're not by my side, I'm incomplete. You both know how much I love you." Brendan's voice was rife with love and commitment—something he warned he'd never be able to give me.

And now I know why.

I'm about to recount the story to my mother when I hear a key in the lock. "Mom? You didn't do something awesome and fly here by chance, did you?"

Her attention is diverted. "No, why."

There's a jiggle of the bottom knob. Swiftly, I move into the kitchen and grab a knife out of the block. "Dad? Jake?"

"Darling, no one. What is happening, Dani?"

The front door creaks open. I whisper, "Because someone just broke in."

"Call 9-1-1!"

Suddenly, there's silence before thundering footsteps rise up the stairs. All thoughts of the knife in my hand disappear. The sharp blade clatters to my feet as I back away from the man facing me with a stricken expression on his face.

"Dani! Are you all right?" my mother shrieks.

"Danielle, give me a chance to explain. Please," Brendan pleads.

I don't know which one I answer when I whisper, "Okay. Fine."

Maybe someday I'll find humor over the fact that they both expelled sighs of relief at the same moment, but not now. Right now, it's taking everything inside of me not to cry and lash out in fury at the expression of devastation on Brendan's face. I murmur a goodbye to my mother before facing my man.

My chin juts out. "How did you know I'd be here?"

"Because you told me the first night we ever came to Nantucket, this is where you come . . ." He swallows hard and barely manages to whisper, "when your life falls apart."

He doesn't make a move to come closer. Neither of us says a word for the longest time before he works up the gumption to say, "You told me you'd never leave, Danielle."

I jerk up my chin. "Who says I walked? Strictly speaking, you left me first when you didn't call me for weeks, Brendan. You left me hanging like a fish on a hook. Then you call and . . ." I can't even finish.

He jams his hand into his back pocket before yanking out the note I left on his kitchen counter, where he'd be sure to find it after he wrapped up the show. "Tell me why," he rasps as he moves forward. Fury and hurt are evident on his face.

They're equally surging through my blood. I don't back down as he approaches. I stand my ground. As he opens his mouth to blow his temper, I shout, "Because I heard you on the bus with your *children*!"

His face pales, but he doesn't correct me. I feel my heart scatter to the four winds. I believed him, trusted him.

That's over.

"You lied to me, Brendan."

His movement abruptly stops before he says, "You didn't understand what you might have overheard."

Scathingly, I repeat, " 'I promise, princess. I love and miss both of you so much.' " I hurl my pain at him, "I thought you didn't know how to love in a way that equated a commitment!"

Brendan's skin turns chalky beneath his tan. He reiterates, "You don't understand."

I back away from him until I reach the door. "I understand I fell in love with a man who has no compunction about lying to me." Then my heart twists inside my chest. "If you'd just trusted me, I wouldn't have cared who their mother is, nor how many children you have. I would have loved them as if they were my own simply because they're yours."

Even as he lunges for me, I throw open the back door and race down the steps toward the beach, seeking somewhere to heal. Or drown.

It doesn't matter which.

CHAPTER THIRTY-FIVE

Brendan

West Moore was seen entering a London theater to attend the opening of Brielle Brogan's newest show on the West End. Afterward, he went backstage and was welcomed by the actress and her husband, financier Patrick Todd.

After the show, he was spotted through the window of his limousine having an intense phone conversation. Do you wonder if he's going to become the next West End angel?

—London Theater Underground

Before I chase after Danielle, I reach into my pocket and pull out my cell. I find a number in my contacts and press call. It rings three times before my father answers. "To what do I owe this pleasure?"

"Are you behind the recent tabloid interest insinuating I've been cheating on Danielle?" I bite out harshly.

I hear a creak as he leans back in his chair. I'm unsurprised to find he's still in his office this late—or early, depending on your perspective. "Did I mention I recently met your beautiful woman at a party?"

Danielle hadn't mentioned any interaction with the infamous software giant who happened to supply half my genes. *Not that we've talked all that much. And that's ending tonight.* I stare intently out the door she disappeared through. Focusing on the bastard taking my time away from fixing my relationship, I query, "Did you?"

"Stunning. More so than they can manage to photograph. Sharp mind. Too bad she's so delusional."

"Shut your fucking mouth, West."

"That woman is adamant about her love for you. Don't tell me you messed it up already?"

"I'll fix Danielle and me. You just stay far away from her."

"Afraid she's going to trade up for money, son?"

"Fuck you, *Dad*. Danielle Madison is more woman than you could ever handle."

"Ah, that sounds like love talking."

"You're damn right. I love her. I love her and am terrified to let her know that."

He scoffs. "What kind of man are you?"

"The kind that was raised by you," I bellow.

I've silenced the great West Moore. Finally, he says, "That's just an excuse."

His words strike a match in the powder keg of my soul.

"If you'd been more of a fucking husband and father, maybe Ursula and Joshua wouldn't feel the need to run away from you at every opportunity. Maybe I'd have a fearless heart instead of one waiting for someone to toss love in my face. Maybe I'd . . ."

I'm interrupted by Danielle's voice ringing out strongly behind me. "Enough, Brendan."

My father takes the opportunity to snark, "Yes, Brendan, run along and—"

"And you? Whoever you are, shut the hell up. Whatever personal value you're trying to elevate by imparting your hatred on Brendan, just stop."

My father's voice drops into a whisper. "I tried to warn you things are not always as they appear, Ms. Madison."

Her eyes narrow on my cell, but I disconnect the call. We're a room apart, and despite my declaration of love, I know her heart's in no way repaired. "Can we talk? Really talk?"

"There's no holding back, Brendan."

"I swear, no more lies. No half-truths."

She turns and walks out the door she came in. I follow her through it and down multiple flights of stairs until we hit the beach. Silently, we walk a short distance before Danielle sits. She looks up at me and tips her head down, saying without words I should join her.

I plop down, wondering if I should start or let her ask questions.

The sun's dipping down over the Atlantic in a fireball of orange and reds, the cooler weather of an early fall shooting flames through the sky. "What did you overhear?"

She shakes her head, and her words don't offer much by way of explanation. "I came in at the tail end when . . . just at the end."

I open my mouth and the words won't come out. Memories of the house in London entwine with images of my mother packing our bags. Seeing the tabloids with my family's faces on them. I cringe. "I don't know where to start."

"Wherever it feels right."

The first thing that flies out of my mouth is, "My biological father is West Moore, software king of the known universe."

The only sound is the crashing of the waves against the sand. Danielle frowns. "I met him recently."

"So he was saying," I grit out.

"He is an unmitigated ass—I'm sorry. Should I say arse?"

I chuckle reluctantly.

"Bet you didn't expect to do that during this talk," she remarks.

"Never in a million years, my queen." I give myself a moment to pull my thoughts together. "West likes his wives young, though he'll take a mistress of any age."

"Charming, Brendan, truly. How did your mother meet him?"

"He was a guest lecturer at the college she was attending. According to her, they 'hit it off.' I try not to ask for too many details. In my mind, she's the Blessed Virgin Mary."

Danielle giggles and the sound lifts some of the oppressive weight I've been hauling around since I found her note. "They were together about a decade—a decade too long, in my opinion."

She scoots closer. "Was he a bad father?"

I give this some serious thought. "He didn't beat me."

"That's the best you can say about him? 'He didn't beat me.' Well, let's go out and get that etched on the Father of the Year award."

I hook an arm around her shoulders and pull her flush against my body. "Okay. That and I didn't exactly grow up wanting for material things."

"And your mother? Was she absent like he was?"

"No. You'll like her."

Danielle tips her head back and arches a brow. I rush to add, "Providing I grovel and take the chance you still want to be a part of my life."

She rests her head on my shoulder. "So, your father is the single richest person on the planet. Why do you hate him?"

"Because of Joshua and Ursula." My response is swift and immediate. Then I clarify, "They're who you heard on the bus."

"Ahh, your 'kids.' Tell me about them."

I do in great detail. I explain how I had cut off all communication with West until I was sixteen and he informed my mother I was getting a sibling. "I felt compelled to talk to the bastard. I wanted to know my brother or sister. Little did I know it would be one of each within a damn year."

Danielle hums her agreement. "Of course you didn't."

I get fired up thinking about it. "He cheated on my mother perpetually. And he divorced Joshua's mother just to make certain he was married to Ursula's so she would be legitimate. What a damn prick."

"We've already established how charming he is. Now, tell me why it mattered so much to you."

"He won't let me see them if it comes out, Danielle."

"If *what* comes out?" Her tone is lethal.

"If it comes out that the three of us are his children, he'll keep Joshua and Ursula from me until they turn eighteen. Then, if they choose to see me after that, they lose their inheritance. They are my family, Danielle. They're a part of me. I'd die to protect the two of them." Silence descends upon us as dusk falls.

Slowly her arm snakes around my back. "I wish I could take my love for you and wrap it around the world to protect all of you from this."

"Danielle." I'm unmanned by the fierceness reflected in her voice.

"This is the man who came storming in to protect me that first night."

My arms tighten around her when I confess, "When I saw that prick manhandling you, all I could think was, what if it was Sula?"

Her head tips back. Damp violet eyes meet mine. "I figured that out. You know what else I've figured out?"

My forehead lowers until it touches hers. "What?"

"It's not that you don't love. It's that you love so selectively because of who that man shaped you to be. No, don't argue." She lays her fingers on my lips when I try to say that nothing good in me exists because of West Moore. "One day, you'll appreciate that gift."

I gently shift her fingers to the side. "That moment isn't right now."

"I didn't think it would be."

I pull her astride me. Her hair falls forward until it forms a shield between us and the world. "Can you forgive me for withholding the truth? Can you understand why I needed to?"

Her fingers trail through my hair, but she takes her time answering. The welling panic I had when I first arrived at her beach house dissipates because as she's taking her time, she's dropping kisses on my forehead, my cheek, the side of my neck. When she finally gets around to answering, my whole body shakes with the force of my emotions at hearing two words escape her lips. "I do."

I thread my fingers in her hair and pull her head back. I kiss her ravenously, my tongue plunging inside and stroking against hers.

Danielle moans and I rip my lips from hers. Burying my face in the curve of her neck, I breathe, "I thought I'd lost you."

Her hands cup the back of my head before she says, "You might have if you didn't come down here and prove me right."

"Prove you right? How?"

Danielle relaxes her body into mine. I feel every slight curve through our clothes. "You love me."

Even though I told her over the phone in order to get her back to Tennessee and shouted them at my father earlier, it's still terrifying to say such impactful words directly to the person who deserves them the most. Finally, I pull her head back down and whisper the words directly against the shell of her ear. "I do. I love you, Danielle."

A sob wrenches from her. I hold on tighter while I give her the truth she earned after the hell I put her through. "I fell in love with you over blueberry and lemon pie, but you knew that already, didn't you? You knew it before you gave me your heart, your soul, and a part of this body no one but me will ever have."

Her head jerks up and down. "Yours. Only yours."

I pull her head back to give her a kiss that vows she has my heart forever, even in this uncertain world.

My heart.

My freedom.

My Dancing Queen.

And, if I'm damn lucky, my future.

CHAPTER THIRTY-SIX

Brendan

Country music star Brendan Blake will appear in a holiday celebrity edition of *Caketastic* on the Food Network for charity.

He'll be baking alongside the elite chefs of the Food Network to raise awareness for the University of Washington Children's Cancer Institute.

He's been very outspoken recently about a family member diagnosed with a rare form of acute myelogenous leukemia. "I feel for the chef paired

up with me. I'm a terrible cook. Just ask my girlfriend," he joked at a press conference.

—Wildcard Music

ONE YEAR LATER

MY KNEE BOUNCES UP AND DOWN SO HARD IT CAUSES MY TEETH TO rattle as I talk with Dani before going out onto the set. "Why did I agree to do something so asinine?"

"Because you're being you?" she mumbles sleepily in my ear. Just her voice is enough to soothe my heart from splintering into a million pieces.

I drop my voice, mindful that anyone could walk into this room unannounced at any moment to drag me in front of the cameras. "I wish I was lying right next to you."

"I'm keeping your pillow warm."

A laugh bursts forth. "You're just hogging all the covers."

I can feel her smile reach across the three thousand miles between us and soothe the ache of my heart. "Guilty. Brendan?"

"Yes, my queen?"

"You're about to humiliate yourself on broadcast television because you'll do anything to make things right for those you love. It's one of the things I love most about you."

Her words choke me up. What did I do to deserve this woman? Where Danielle could have so easily run away from us, she held on. She claims I'm her storm, but if I am, it's because I need her by my side to power through the trials life throws at us both—like finding out my second cousin, my "nephew" who has always called me "Uncle" Brendan due to our age difference, has a rare form of cancer. *Christ, can life cut us a fucking break?* Needing to remind us both of the blessings we've been gifted, I murmur, "I love you too."

"I know."

"Besides, you're right. Who really cares if I burn a cake into oblivion?"

That's when a sultry southern voice drawls from behind me, "I do, considering it's my reputation that's going to be on that line."

I spin on my heel and find myself face-to-face with a woman who can only be described as stunning. The rest of her must set most men's tongues flapping out of their mouths. The newcomer is curvaceous, with exotic features, eyes of gold, and hair that reminds me of chocolate and caramel swirled together. Her lips lift in an amused tilt that lets me know she holds no regret about listening in on the last part of my call.

Danielle laughs in my ear, breaking me from my perusal. "I assume your chef just showed up?"

"I haven't introduced myself yet." Tucking the phone beneath my chin, I stick out a hand. "Brendan Blake. I'm just wrapping up a call."

She takes it before her simple honesty causes my jaw to drop. "Corinna. I'd have to be dead not to know who you are, Mr. Blake. You're one of my family's favorite musicians."

Stunned stupid, I nearly forget everything that was in my briefing about the chefs. "I'm sorry. I don't recognize your name from the packet the network sent over."

A smile crosses her lips. "I'm Corinna Freeman. One of the chefs is out due to illness, and they asked me—a huge honor, mind you—to step in. I'm part owner of Amaryllis Events in Collyer, Connecticut. I run the—"

Before Corinna can finish, there's a deafening bellow as my no longer sleepy girlfriend shouts, "Put me on speaker. Now, Brendan!"

Fumbling with my phone, I apologize to the chef in her pristine white jacket, jeans, and—to my amusement—neon-orange Chucks. "My girlfriend, Danielle, would like to . . ."

Before I can make an excuse, Dani is shouting, "Corinna? Emily's sister?"

Love for her family illuminates the woman in front of me even further. Her lips curve so widely that I'm gobsmacked. Christ, she's a knockout. "One and the same."

"Holy crap, Brendan. You're not just going on television. You're about to endure boot camp," Danielle outright snickers.

Corinna's not the least bit insulted, though she does tap a finger against her lips. "I will deny Em my caramel sauce for a year for spreading such lies about me."

Suddenly, the easy camaraderie between my love and the woman in front of me clicks. "Hold on, Dani. Your Em and Corinna are . . ."

"Sisters," Corinna confirms. "And call me Cori."

"Cori, I'm so disappointed I haven't had a chance to meet you." The springs on the other end squeak as Dani shifts, now completely awake.

Her head cocks to the side. "Meet me? Oh, that's right, you came to see Em the day I was triple booked." Her eyes glint with malice. "Cassidy's still making people pay for that. And by people, I mean Phillip."

"I imagine so," Dani snickers. "Do you know the picture of you wearing the gold dress is the basis for my first custom-made red-carpet dress?"

Corinna braids her hair and smiles in amusement as Dani concludes their side conversation with, "Emily talks about all of you all the time."

Corinna finishes with her long braid and ties it off. "The six of us are closer than the average siblings."

My jaw unhinges. "Six? Six sisters?"

"No, the oldest is Phillip. We cut him some slack in the sanity department because he raised five younger sisters."

Five younger sisters? "He deserves a medal."

"Something my brothers-in-law have remarked on," Corinna jokes.

"If I had five sisters, I need to be nominated for a lobotomy, let alone sainthood." The idea of four more Sulas running around the world causes my stomach to pitch and roll.

We're still laughing when a head pops in.

"Mr. Blake? Ms. Freeman? Fifteen minutes." They duck out just as quickly.

Corinna murmurs a goodbye to Dani before she steps away with a flimsy excuse to give us some privacy. I take Dani off speaker before joking, "Well, when I drown, at least it will be with a friendly face."

"Brendan, if even half the stories Em has told me about her family are true, you're in great hands," Dani reassures me before she yawns.

"Go back to sleep, baby."

"Just for a few hours. I'm heading to the hospital in the morning."

"I love you, Dancing Queen."

"I love you, Honky Tonk." She disconnects the call. With my back to the center of the room, defeat at letting Joey down yawns before me.

Corinna's voice washes over me. "Tell me about who we're battling for."

"Joey?"

"Yes."

I turn and find her half a room away. I pull up the photos stored on my phone and I warn her, "These pictures aren't easy to look at."

"A lot of life's moments are like that."

I flip to the most recent picture I have of me and Joey. They were taken in his hospital room in Seattle. My voice sounds strangled when I inform the young chef, "I'd give up my music career if I knew he'd get better."

"And that's why he's still fighting. He's fighting not just for himself but for everyone who loves him." My head snaps up, but I see she's memorizing the photo. Her words come from a part of her soul I'm not even certain she knows she's exposing. "Everyone has moments they prefer to forget. Inevitably, when they're examined, it's knowing who stood with them that gentles the memory."

While I'm still absorbing her words, I feel a gentle grip on my shoulder. "Mr. Blake?"

I give her a brief smile. "Corinna, please. Call me Brendan."

Her lips curve before she pins me with a question. "How well do you take orders?"

"According to my band," *and my father,* I amend silently. "Not well at all. Why?"

"Because if you want to win as much as I do, you have to do everything I tell you. And if you don't understand, say so upfront. Because we're going to win for that little boy." She nods at the phone I'm still clutching in my hand. "And we're going to have a blast in the process to show him his uncle's doing this for him."

I tip my head down toward her and say in a voice laced with disbelief, "You think you can beat the best the Food Network is going to throw at us?"

She tosses her long braid over her shoulder. "I don't think it, I know it. And when *we* win, we'll bake your nephew a cake for you to bring home to celebrate with."

"FIVE MINUTES!" is shouted outside the closed door. But I can't drag my eyes away from the determination on Corinna Freeman's face. "I don't know why I believe you, but I do."

"Good." She strides to the door and flings it open. "Let's get to work."

I crawl into bed with Dani sixteen hours later, holding a piece of quadruple chocolate cake that Corinna Freeman concocted—with my half-assed assistance—to win *Caketastic.*

I'm exhausted but I need to wake up the only person in the world who can read me and without me breaking the non-disclosure agreements I signed regarding the results of today's competition.

Shaking Dani's shoulder, I rumble, "Wake up, Dancing Queen. I have something for you."

Her face is smashed into my pillow, I note with amusement. "Can't it wait till morning, Honky—" Her body goes rigid. When she shoots up in bed, she almost upends the cake I carried across the country on my lap. "How did it go?"

I look down at the plate and murmur, "I brought you a piece of the winning cake."

"Oh?" She pulls it from my hands.

I lift my eyes and don't give a shit that tears are falling down my cheeks. "It's called *Joey's Justice.*"

Dani's lip trembles. Carefully, she places the plate on the nightstand. Then she wraps herself around me while I let loose the heaving emotions swirling around me all day. "You did it," she whispers.

"No, it was all Corinna. She did something completely incomprehensible."

"What's that, my love?"

I swallow a few times as I recall the stories Corinna Freeman dredged from me as she confidently moved around the kitchen. Even when I thought we were done for, she never stopped fighting. "She taught me there are different ways to communicate love." I tip Dani's head back and brush my lips against hers with intent.

Dani slides her hands beneath my shirt and whispers, "Show me."

I don't need to be asked twice. I lay her back and push my tee over her head. In between gasps and sighs, I hitch her leg up over my hip and slide in until the heat of her wraps around me.

At one point, I look down into her face. I feel my chest open wide at her love beaming up at me. Dropping my head, I kiss Danielle knowing her heart is where my home is, where we're going to build our lives.

I now know it's time I introduce the ghosts of my past to the blinding light of my future.

CHAPTER THIRTY-SEVEN

Brendan

Wildcard Music is closed from now until after the first of the year as a bonus to all our employees. This year, we want to gift our employees time with their families.

Those who are mission-critical will be granted an equal amount of time after January 3rd.

In the last few months, we've all learned there's nothing more precious than the ability to be with our loved ones.

—Internal memo from Kristoffer Wilde to all Wildcard Music Employees

---

DECEMBER

I'M SO HAPPY TO HAVE THE KIDS AT MY SIDE AFTER THE LAST THREE months of madness in the world, I don't care that JB's giving me a British history lesson. "Boxing Day originated in Great Britain as a day to give gifts to those in need or in a position of service. The tradition dates back to the Middle Ages but has a great tie to an older British tradition where the servants of the wealthy were allowed the day after Christmas to visit their families since they would have had to serve the ton on Christmas Day." He lifts his paper cup filled with tea to his lips and takes a sip before sneering at the plastic lid.

"Be grateful it's hot, kid."

He rolls his eyes.

Sula scoffs from the back of my extended cab, "It's a bunch of rubbish now, B. From everything I've been told—even by Father's servants—it's basically equivalent to America's Black Friday. And thank you for my caramel macchiato. It's delicious."

I grin in the rearview mirror. "You're welcome, princess. I figured you both would need something after the flight. It couldn't have been easy to get on a plane . . . after." For once—and maybe the only time ever—I actually understood West's reluctance to allow the kids to visit me.

Christ, the world's a holy mess. I feel more than a twinge of selfishness for bringing them here, but according to West, "They want to be with you. I will do everything within my power to ensure they travel safely to do so, Brendan. Treat them like precious cargo."

More shocking than the words he used to describe them, my father arranged undercover guards to fly over with my brother and sister. It might be the most compassionate thing he's ever done. I have to give him credit for the fatherly gesture, though it pains me to do so.

"Like I said, we have a big day ahead of us."

213

Bigger than either of them could imagine.

"Are we going somewhere?" JB asks curiously.

"No, we're staying at home."

"Are Glenda and Smith coming over?" Sula asks eagerly.

"Later tonight." Danielle persuaded me it would be a good idea to have a family dinner tonight after she's met the kids. "Brendan, despite the fact they're almost sixteen—"

"JB is sixteen," I corrected her.

"Still, you have to think about their reactions. Teenagers are unusual creatures . . . stop laughing!"

"I'm sorry, my queen. It's just you sound like a mother already." I tugged her into my lap.

She wrapped her arms around my neck before nodding at Jenna who was fighting with Jake over where to hang lights. "I know of what I speak. You don't spring a surprise like this without reassuring the kids nothing fundamental is going to change."

That's when I speared my hand into Danielle's hair and kissed her until Jenna yelled, "Get a room!"

Now, we're driving back from the airport. "Christ, I need to fly you both here on private planes from now on. That was a hot mess at the airport."

"You're telling me. I mean, I knew you were popular, but this?" says JB.

Sula drawls from the back, "Such a hardship, B. Let me ponder how hard that will be to get used to. Okay. I'm done. Can we fly home that way?"

JB mutters, "Right?" as he reads something on his phone, some other bit of British history he feels it's imperative I know.

I think back to my mother's text earlier. She's lovely. I can't wait to meet her tonight.

> **Brendan**
> You called her?

My text was immediately replied to.

> **Mom**
> Yes! We talked for about an hour. What is taking you so long?

I groaned before replying.

> **Brendan**
> Don't ask. The airport is a madhouse.

> **Mom**
> You should have let Smith get them, darling.

> **Brendan**
> Back to Danielle.

> **Mom**
> I was prepared to like her for you.
>
> If she's that lovely in person, I'm ready to love her.

We're a few miles from the house when I broach the subject. I pull to the side of the road and put the car in park. "Let's talk."

I immediately have both of their attention. I shift in my seat so my back is to the door and I can see their faces. Taking a deep breath, I just come clean. "I've fallen in love. I need you both to know what I have with Danielle is forever."

I don't realize Sula's undone her belt and has leaned over the seat to grab one of my hands.

"If you would give her a chance, she's just waiting to open up her enormous heart to both of you too."

"You finally told her about us?" JB asks warily.

I clasp his shoulder. "And can't wait to meet you."

Sula chews her lip uncertainly. "Are you certain, B? I mean, we don't mean to be, but we're a bit of a handful."

"Sula, you are loved." My eyes pin JB in place. "You both are."

"And your Dani accepts this?"

"More than. In fact, I almost lost her over it."

"What?" they shout in unison.

I wince. "Well, she accidentally overheard us talking on the bus the last time you were here. We"—I gesture between the three of us—"had to agree that I could tell her, so I kept the two of you a secret. I lied by omission and she abhors liars."

"Damn right, she does!" Sula says indignantly.

"Sula, mouth," I warn.

She glares at me mutinously, offended on behalf of a woman she hasn't even met yet. Since that happens to be the woman I'm in love with, I let it slide. One side of my lips lifts before I tell them, "She thought you were my children. She said there was so much adoration in our voices. It's something she's only seen in close parent and child relationships."

Abruptly, JB yanks out of my reach. "I want to meet her."

"Me too. Is she at the house?" Sula asks. She flops backward and snaps on her seatbelt.

"Yes. She also arranged for Mama and Smith to come over later . . ." I need not have spoken.

JB reaches over and prods me in the shoulder. "Let me drive so I can get in some practice."

"Absolutely not, the roads aren't completely clear." I put the truck in gear and ease back onto the road. To ensure they're all right, I clarify, "I know we agreed to let Danielle know, but I need to make certain you both are okay with this."

"Can you drive faster than an old woman, B? Maybe then we'll get to meet your Dani before you turn forty." Sula taunts sweetly after I edge up to a four-way stop.

JB howls with laughter.

"You two are a pain in my ass most days."

"Yes, but you love us," Sula declares. "And now we have more family, don't we?"

I slam on the brakes at the base of my driveway. "That's how you look at it?"

JB frowns. "Don't you?"

I swallow over and over, trying to shift the knot from my throat. "Yeah, buddy. That's exactly how I view it."

The phone rings in the car. I check the caller ID and put it on speaker. My voice still husky, I call out, "Hey, Dancing Queen."

"Honky Tonk, if you don't tell me what to put out for your brother and sister for munchies, I'm killing you the minute you come through the door." Danielle's in full panic mode.

I grin at the wonderment on JB and Sula's faces. That's when Sula blurts, "Can I have a peanut butter and jelly sandwich? I only get them when I'm at B's."

"Me too? Only can you make mine with Fluff?" JB asks.

There's a quick pause before Dani replies, "As a bonus, after we kill your older brother for my meltdown being on speaker, we can share the Christmas cookies I made . . . what's that sound?"

"Me bottoming out because I sped up. We're at the bottom of the driveway, my queen. You didn't say jack about baking."

"That's because I've been in a panic, Brendan!"

"We left your mother's cookies at her house." I pull up to the semi-circular driveway just in time to see the front door open. Danielle leans against the jamb in a horrific Christmas sweater that comes to her thighs paired with leggings.

Before she hangs up, her eyes meet mine through the windshield as she taunts, "And who do you think I learned to bake from?"

Then she runs to the truck in her stocking feet—exactly the same way she greeted Jake and Jenna just a few days before at her parent's home in upstate New York. By the time I've rounded the hood, Dani's head is whipping back and forth between JB's and Sula's faces. Both kids are staring at her with something akin to awe. It isn't until I sling an arm around each of their shoulders and prompt her with a "Well?" that Danielle moves.

And what she does binds her to them both for life. She opens her arms wide enough to embrace both Sula and JB, completing our circle. Her head falls forward until it's touching mine before she greets them. "Welcome home, kids."

We stay like that for a few moments until JB mutters, "Shit."

I rear back. "What?"

Sula has kept hold of Danielle and has an arm hooked around her waist. Both have quizzical expressions on their faces.

"I just realized the worst part of our family expanding."

Danielle frowns. "There's a bad part?"

"There is when your new sister is the most gorgeous woman in the world and you're going to have to listen to your mates go off about how hot she is. I won't have a leg to stand on when I beat them bloody!" JB shouts.

Sula croons, "Isn't that sweet."

"Have you told B about the guy who asked you out?"

I swear all the blood drains from my face. "No. Just, no."

Sula sneers. "Now you sound like *him*. It's just a study date. At a *library*."

The three of us bicker on our way into the house. Just as I'm about to cross into the foyer, I realize Danielle isn't with me. I call out, "Don't kill each other," before racing back to where she's standing with a bemused expression on her gorgeous face. I tug her body against mine before asking, "What is it?"

"How is it possible you gave me even more love?"

"Danielle," I murmur. My hands shift over her back.

Her voice is filled with wonder. "It's a gift, an honor. I knew I loved you, that I would love them, but I never expected it to happen in an instant. How did I never predict this?"

"You're the damn miracle," I tell her, before I kiss her out in the cool air.

I don't let her up until I hear Sula shout, "If you eat all the cookies, B is going to hurt you, JB!"

I pull back with a smile on my lips. Dani leans into me as we make our way up the walk. "Your mother called me a little while ago. How did she have my number?"

"I gave it to her." I grin when I feel Danielle bash her head against my shoulder.

"A heads-up would have been nice. I think I stuttered through the call." Before I can tell her what my mother said, she tips her head back and her smile turns wonky.

I follow her gaze upward and find the mistletoe she insisted upon hanging in the foyer. "Well, we can't break tradition."

Then I fill my soul with the only present I'll ever need—Danielle in my arms.

CHAPTER THIRTY-EIGHT

Danielle

Country music star Brendan Blake put on one hell of a show in Connecticut tonight. He called *Caketastic* baking partner Corinna Freeman up on stage. The two have remained fast friends with the Amaryllis Events team sending donations to the University of Washington Cancer Research Institute in honor of Joey Blake.

Blake's girlfriend, supermodel Danielle Madison, was spotted backstage with close friends of Blake's. She was not only sporting her infamous ear-to-ear

grin, but she was wearing a STORM T-shirt and her beloved John Deere cap.

—New York Entertainment

"What's happening, Dani?" Sula asks as she and JB sidle up beside me backstage.

Smith winks as he weaves his way to the other side to help with the special guest Brendan's about to call up on stage.

We're in Connecticut for the night and all the Freeman siblings are in the pit—including my Emily, Brendan's Corinna. They, along with a few of their assorted family and friends, are joining us backstage after the show is over.

Brendan plans on spotlighting Corinna tonight. Joey's been giving him regular reports on the sheer volume of cupcakes Corinna and the Amaryllis team have sent each week. "They're so good, Uncle Brendan."

"Don't make me jealous, kid. The last time I had any of Cori's cakes was the night of *Caketastic*."

That same week, Corinna whipped together blueberry cupcakes with lemon curd filling and cream cheese frosting for me to take to Brendan on the road. At Brendan's astounded, "How the hell did she manage this?" I let him in on the secret. "I might have asked Em if she'd mind. Corinna baked, I was merely the delivery person."

He shoved the box to the side and stretched me out on top of the table. "Cori's cupcakes are fantastic, but you, my love, surpass them."

We didn't devour them for hours.

Tonight, as I wait in the wings with JB's arm around me and his sister, Brendan sings and plays with his whole heart. The air rises with the tempo of his music. Not a single person in the audience is quiet as he works them into a frenzy.

Pride swells up and overflows when he ends the number and he rumbles into the mic, "As you might have seen, I have some special guests tonight. She's going to kill me for doing this, but I'd like to bring one up on stage."

From the safety of the wings, I see the Freeman clan lose their minds in the pit as Brendan's security team escorts Corinna onto the stage. She's just as stunning as she was in that gold dress I spotted in Emily's portfolio. When she's within touching distance, Brendan holds out his hand. Corinna takes it, but she's unprepared for when he tugs her forward for an embrace. With my own set of earwigs in, I hear him murmur, "There are not enough ways to say thank you for everything, Cori."

She wraps her arms around his neck and squeezes him. "It's been my pleasure, B."

Then Corinna squeals when Brendan lifts her and spins around in circles. Her head arches back and her hair fans out. JB sucks in a breath so harshly next to me, I'm certain all the air backstage has just been inhaled into his lungs. I nudge him to get his attention. "She's too old for you."

"Doesn't keep a guy from fantasizing, Dani," he retorts.

I slap a hand over my mouth so I don't giggle too loudly. Just then, Brendan leans over into his mic and says, "Thanks, Cori. Thank for doing what you did, for being who you are to me, and to everyone who knows your heart."

Knowing what I do from Smith, I can't wait to finally meet this woman who has earned a special place in my man's heart.

"God, she's even more gorgeous close up," JB moans.

Sula elbows him in the stomach.

We're at the far side of the massive tent that's been guarded all during the show. Brendan's finished with his normal after show meet and greet with his fans and is on his way. Meanwhile, the tide of people just parted. My eyes are locked on Corinna Freeman's.

I can't wait for Brendan any longer.

I break away from the kids and saunter toward Corinna. She hands her glass to one of her sisters. The minute I'm within arm's reach, I lay a hand on her shoulder and tug her forward.

Corinna steps willingly into my embrace.

We rock back and forth for long minutes without saying a word until I hear Emily grumble, "What the hell am I? Chop suey?"

That's when I get an enormous insight into the Freeman family. Corinna steps back and dashes her fingers under her eyes before pleading, "You can be it, but for the love of god, don't try to make it."

Holly, the red-haired titan, removes the camera from her face and chimes in. "We all like to live, Em."

Cassidy's brilliant aqua eyes sparkle when she agrees. "Em, you cook as poorly as you sing. "

Emily shrugs as if it makes no never mind all her sisters are calling her out.

"Darling, that's why we kept telling you to hush during the show," says her brother.

Emily's look turns lethal. "No, Phillip, that's because they wanted to chastise you for tossing a bra on stage. For Christ's sake. Neon orange? Where in the hell did you find that?"

I raise my hand.

Both Emily and Corinna inform me, "Don't bother being polite." And "Just jump in."

I shrug before lowering it and ask Phillip, "Where *did* you find it? If you haven't heard, I love everything Day-Glo."

Phil chokes on his beer, causing the circle of women to laugh. "Em will kill me if I tell you."

"Damn straight, I will," Emily threatens.

"You're a blood-thirsty bunch," I note.

"Only with each other. Only for each other. To us, family is everything," Corinna clarifies.

"I completely agree."

"How's Joey?" Corinna asks.

I launch into detail about the newest treatment they're trying. Corinna asks a few questions, including whether she should be sending so many cupcakes. I smirk. "I think the nurses are intercepting them now. Don't you worry about that."

She laughs. "Good to know."

Just as I'm about to expound on how Brendan's nephew is faring, we all hear a piercing whistle and turn in its direction. My heart and other body parts rev up when I see Brendan tuning an acoustic guitar. "Hey, Cori! If my woman is done yakking your ear off, how about y'all come on down here for a moment."

"Oh, hell. No, he isn't."

"Come on, Corinna," I coax.

I slip an arm around her shoulders, but she digs in her heels. Literally. She tries to use them to anchor herself in place. "There's not a chance in hell I'm being serenaded."

"I could guilt you into it," I warn her quietly.

She tosses her gorgeous locks. "Impossible."

I find it adorable that Corinna Freeman, the underdog who kicked Food Network ass and had no problem sauntering on stage in front of 20,000 fans, has to be dragged by me to sit next to Brendan.

He waits for the room to get silent before briefly recapping the day he and Corinna met. Then he faces her. "It's rare when you find someone who makes magic just by existing. A person who brightens your day with just a smile."

Corinna blushes. "Brendan, please. This isn't necessary."

"It is for me, so hush your mouth."

Corinna bites her lower lip but remains silent.

Brendan continues. "The woman sitting next to me wasn't born into a family that appreciated her, but she found one that did."

Even from my vantage point standing behind Brendan's shoulder, I can see Corinna's eyes start to fill.

"You tell her, Brendan!" her sister Alison shouts.

"I plan on doing better than that, Ali." Brendan strums his guitar. The room inhales collectively, me included. "Anyone here ever hear of an amazing songwriter named Toby Lightman?"

"Oh God," Corinna whimpers.

I cross behind them and squeeze Corinna's shoulders, partially in support. In large part to keep her in place to accept Brendan's gift.

"Before a compassionate hand drags you out of the hardest moments of your life, you sometimes forget how to do this." That's when the love of my life starts serenading this woman who, if the trembling beneath my fingers is any indication, has layers of fear hidden beneath her veneer of confidence.

While he's been practicing this song, Brendan told me about why the artist wrote it. "The song's about how she had to move on and continue fighting. Isn't that what Corinna helped me do for Joey?"

Now, I think back to Brendan's wastrel father and nod. This woman, this incandescent woman, did more than Midas himself could when presented with the chance. I lean down and wrap my arms around Corinna from behind. We sway together as he continues to use the power of his voice to dispel any doubt about his appreciation for what Corinna did for him then.

And the fight she continues to battle alongside him.

My eyes lock with Sula's. She's wrapped in JB's arms next to Glenda and Smith. Glenda's holding up the phone so her sister, Edolie, can let Joey watch "Uncle Brendan" from the other side of the country.

Even as the lights of the tent twinkle above us, I know they, too, have turned into magic.

Love, in its purest form, has a way of doing that.

CHAPTER THIRTY-NINE

Danielle

We're pleased to announce the engagement of Brendan Blake to Danielle Madison. As you are likely aware, the couple first met at the *Incandescence* party in New York over a year ago.

They've been inseparable ever since.

On behalf of everyone at Wildcard Music, we offer them every happiness.

—Paula Stone, Wildcard Music Media Representative

BRENDAN BENDS HIS KNEES BENEATH MINE AND KISSES THE BACK of my neck. "Did Sula and JB have a good time tonight?"

I tip my head to the side when his lips travel down the column of my neck. We're at home in our bedroom in Nashville. Sula and JB pestered their father enough to spend their winter holiday with us. The four of us spent the day over at Glenda and Smith's. Tonight we hung out in the screening room of our new home—Nashville now being my base of operations.

I'm in New York often enough that I get time with my Phina and to feed my addiction to all clothes designed by Emily Freeman. Besides, with the way Brendan and I travel, every second we have together is precious.

The splash it made in the papers was insane. I grumbled to Brendan, "You think we solved world peace instead of cohabitating."

He held up his hands and teased, "Listen, if they want to give me a Nobel Peace Prize for being the smartest man alive, I'm okay with that."

"Smartest man alive? What makes you think that?"

"Well, I did fall in love with you."

It's easier to protect Sula and JB now. A runway was one of the first things Brendan had built on the new property. "I don't care how much money it costs. I am going to lessen their exposure to protect them."

"I completely agree. They deserve to be kids for as long as possible."

For now, West Moore's secret remains just that—a secret. "Though you should know I overheard JB talking to one of his mates. He told him about how Corinna sent him a box of baked goods. His little crush on Corinna isn't abating."

Brendan stops kissing my neck to mutter, "He needs to crush on someone who's not in a committed relationship."

"That's almost what I said to him verbatim. Then, after he hung up, he asked if I knew of anyone. I told him I'd think about it right before I stole *our* box of Corinna goodies out of his hands. "

"Excellent job protecting our baked goods, my queen."

I smile in the dark. "I do my best."

His hand drifts down over my stomach and rests there. "One day, are you going to teach our children how to love so openly?"

Every muscle in my body locks. I stutter, "Our . . . our children?"

He scoots away from me, which is absolutely the last thing I want at this moment. Fortunately for my pounding heart, it's only long enough for Brendan to roll me to my back before he covers my body with his. His hazel eyes bore into mine before he repeats, "Ours. Yours and mine."

My breath hitches. "You're serious."

He lowers himself so he can brace his torso on one forearm. He picks up my left hand and while staring at me, lifts it to brush his lips over my trembling fingers. "I've never been more serious about anything in my life."

"But you said . . ." I clamp my mouth shut.

Brendan leans over and brushes his lips against mine. "The man who spewed that nonsense was still reacting to being hurt as a child by what some may call a parent."

I swallow around the lump in my throat, willing him to continue.

"Part of me will never stop feeling sorry for that boy or his mother. Neither of them had a chance to experience a loving home."

I cup his cheek, my fingers spreading over his beard. His next words still my movement.

"But that boy turned into a man. A man who was blessed with a gift—a love where the freedom I sought is where we soar together. I only achieve it when I'm wrapped in your arms each night."

I map out the features of his face before I say, "I love you, Brendan."

"I love you, Danielle. You are under each layer of my skin, buried deep in my heart." He reaches past me for the drawer of the end table. Yanking it open, he pulls out a small velvet box. He clasps it in his palm for a moment before he sits up and then tugs me until I'm straddling his lap. "And I know I want the rest of eternity with you."

He cracks the box and I gape at the three-stone ring with a large purple cushion cut stone holding court in the center. "Brendan," I wheeze.

"Marry me, Danielle." He plucks the ring out of the box and holds it over the third finger of my left hand.

My lips tremble but somehow I say, "You had the answer the first night you touched me. Please."

Brendan slips the ring on my finger before he wraps me up in his arms and flips me backward until he looms over me in our bed. He growls, "Let me see if I can get you to shriek it again."

Sliding my leg along the outside of his, I press a kiss to the underside of his chin. "I'm perfectly fine with that."

Hours later, body limp from every emotion Brendan managed to wring out of it, I realize he is right. We soar higher together than when we're apart. I curl against him, and his arms tighten. Yes, we found our definition of being free.

And, as my eye catches the purple sapphire and diamonds screaming Brendan's commitment to me, it's also the perfect definition of love.

CHAPTER FORTY

Danielle

Recently named Country's Sexiest Bachelor and look what happens? Brendan Blake is off the market!

He married his longtime girlfriend, Danielle Madison, at a private beach ceremony this past weekend.

Attended by family and a few close friends, the couple shared the following details about their nuptials. Danielle's dress was an Amaryllis Design

original. Professional photographs of the happy couple were captured by celebrity photographer Phina Hart. In lieu of wedding cake, the couple served blueberry lemon pie.

No one who attended the ceremony is talking, but a member of the waitstaff said the now Mrs. Brendan Blake slipped a gift into her husband's pocket at the altar that brought him to tears.

Could she be pregnant already?

—Nashville Nights

SEPTEMBER

"I'M GOING TO CRY," MY MOTHER CLAIMS FOR THE FIFTIETH TIME as she slides the tiny zipper up my back. My wedding gown is constructed of an almost mesh-like lace, with Emily's meticulous hand beadwork adding just enough sparkle to pick up the glitter of the sun sparkling off the ocean.

I twirl. "It's so airy, it's almost effortless to wear." The full skirt floats away from my legs and bare feet that are adorned with nothing more than a French pedicure.

Phina snaps one shot after another. "That dress is timeless."

I glance down at the sleeves that cling yet drape so effortlessly. "You think so?"

"Yes." Phina puts her camera down and approaches me to fuss with my curls before she narrows her eyes in critique. "That's because your happiness is going to be. Emily has a way of translating that. Twenty years from now, you're going to remember this moment and realize nothing's changed, Dancing Queen."

"One thing will have," I contradict.

"What's that, Dani?" My mother asks.

"I'll love Brendan more than I do today." That's when I hear the click of the camera. Phina and I turn to see Glenda—taking a picture of the three of us.

"What? It was too perfect of a picture to pass up."

My smile fades as I gaze out the window. Brendan, I know, is getting ready in the apartment over the garage with Jake and rock god, Beckett Miller. I mean, he'd mentioned his friend Beckett, but I had no idea the two were as close as they were until he told me about how Beckett worked for Small Town Nights until he, too, was discovered by Kristoffer Wilde.

Glenda stands behind me and rests her hand on my shoulder. "You tried your hardest."

"I know but it hurts me that any part of today is causing him distress." On what should be the happiest day of our lives, our wedding day, it's partially marred because of the douchebag that donated half of Brendan's genes. He's mourning the fact his younger brother and sister won't be at the wedding because, *"It's your choice to marry . . . your model after the school year begins."*

"Oh, come on, West," Brendan protested.

"They are not legal adults, Brendan. Should they—or you—make an attempt for them to leave the country, it will not be pleasant for any of you." He hung up on his oldest son at that point.

Like JB and Sula, the rest of us who are in the know are devastated they won't see Brendan marry. He promised them we'd repeat the wedding in person whenever they wanted. Sula moaned, *"It won't be the same."*

No, it won't be the same, I agree privately. Shaking off my maudlin mood, I whirl around and ask, "How much more time?"

"Just a few—" Phina begins. There's a sudden knock at the door. She frowns. "Who is that?"

"Well, we know it's not Brendan." Glenda points out the window.

My head whips around and my jaw falls open at how handsome he is wearing his minimalist ensemble—dark blue shirt, matching slacks and jacket. The first button is left open and his head's bare. *So I can run my fingers through his hair when I kiss him,* I think dreamily.

"I say, do you hear me, Dani?" comes a lightly accented voice that sounds a million miles away yet is right next to me.

Cautiously, I turn. I'm fearful of getting my hopes up. That's when Caleb Lockwood—who happens to be the co-owner of Hudson Investigations—holds out a phone to me. His expression is carefully blank. Completely different from when he arrived with his wife, sisters-in-law, and brother-in-law, Colby Hunt. Instead, he explains blandly, "This call came in on your fiancé's personal line. Since he's on his way down to the ceremony, Smith said you should take it."

I wait for Caleb to leave the room and ask for everyone else to give me a moment of privacy before I whisper, "Are you here?"

"Give me a break, Dani. I cut class. I didn't manage to fly across an ocean." Sula's voice penetrates the air.

That's when another voice breaks in. "Sod it, I couldn't manage to sneak off campus. I tried a couple of times. Got some cheek because of it. Bloody buggers called West."

Sula talks to her brother. "Did you get in trouble, JB?"

"No more than usual, Sula," he reassures her.

I interrupt them. "What are you two doing?"

"Glenda said she'd take pictures and text them to us," Sula announces.

"But we decided we're going to do one better," JB proclaims.

"We're going to listen in. Glenda will hold us for the ceremony. West can't stop us from doing that." Disgust fills Sula's voice with even the briefest mention of her father.

An overwhelming aura of peace settles over me. My gown swishing around my legs, I stride over to the table and pick up my bouquet. "I've got one better."

"Oh?" Sula's curious.

"Do you trust me?"

"Absolutely," JB declares.

"Then how would you both like to take a walk with me?" I tuck the small phone behind the massive bouquet Phillip Freeman sent upstairs. I tell them of the spur-of-the-moment idea I have planned. "You both are going to have to be on mute," I warn.

"We can do that!" Sula screeches.

"Oh, bloody brilliant," JB agrees.

"Do it now," I urge them both. I wait until there's complete silence before I turn the screen black and step from the master suite to find a row of the most important women in my life waiting.

My mom and aunt had better be grateful they're wearing waterproof makeup. My niece Jenna's deep brown eyes—an exact replica of her father's—are shining. I smile widely recalling Jake's reaction to Jenna opening her attendant's gift last night at the rehearsal dinner—a brand new Louis Vuitton handbag. His "For the love, Dani!" roared over the sound of the ocean.

As did Jenna's squeal of delight.

Toward the end of the gaggle of women, Emily's eyeing her creation critically. She's become my exclusive designer and, oh, so much more.

And of course, standing at my back, prodding me forward, capturing my joy, is my Phina.

Taking a deep breath, I announce, "It's time."

I'm grateful there isn't a peep from the phone in my hands.

At least not now.

There's about fifty people between our family and close friends at our wedding, many of whom are staying at the house or at the rentals on either side of my home in Sconset. As I walk on my father's arm down the beach toward Brendan, they could all disappear, and it wouldn't matter.

All that matters is the man waiting for me at the end of the aisle under an arbor anchored in blueberries, lemons, hydrangeas, and lavender. It's a theme echoed in my bouquet and in the enormous vases holding down the runner on the beach.

I catch sight of Brendan and thank God I already planned on how I was going to tell Brendan his siblings *are* actually at our wedding because the vision of him waiting at the end of the aisle with my cousin and Beckett Miller standing at his side almost does me in. Especially when I catch sight of the tears falling down his cheeks.

Halfway through our procession, my father mutters, "At least you had the good sense not to bother with a veil, Dani. No doubt, it'd be in the ocean. Besides, then I wouldn't be able to do this." My father spins me out, almost causing me to drop the phone.

I toss my head back and laugh as he spins me back. The audience roars at the impromptu move.

My father grins at me. "Much better. Now I won't sob like a little baby handing you over to Brendan—not that he hasn't been a member of this family for ages."

"Dad?"

"Yes, baby?"

"I'm so happy. I love him so much." I say the words as much for my father as I do for his siblings.

"I know, sweetheart. It's written all over you."

We approach the end of the aisle. That's when my eyes connect with Brendan's. His are glowing. I wait for my father to answer, "Her mother and I do," to the minister.

I deviate from what we practiced yesterday—pausing before handing my flowers back to my maid of honor. Stepping so close to Brendan I can feel the brush of his jacket against my bare amrs, I murmur, "You look so happy, Honky Tonk."

His smile is full of joy. "I'm marrying you, Dancing Queen. Of course, I'm happy."

"Do you remember when you proposed you said you deserved a Nobel Peace Prize for being the smartest man alive?"

His lips curve sensuously. "Of course I do. I was about to ask you to marry me."

Then I move my lips to his ear and whisper, "I'm about to oust you from that spot."

"How's that?"

I use my bouquet to block my hand slipping his phone into his pocket. "I'm about to give you Moore."

He visibly jolts when his pocket vibrates as I say words that cue the kids so they can send their brother texts at exactly the same moment. Casually I add, "Your phone rang when we were both getting ready. Caleb brought it to me. *Very* important people on the other end who wanted to be with us today. "

He jerks his head back before he pieces it together. His forehead crashes against mine. He barely manages to choke out my name. "Danielle."

I lower my eyes deliberately to his pocket. "They plan on being with us all night."

His breath catches. I say slightly louder, "I love you, Honky Tonk."

"I'll always love you, my queen."

I turn and pass my flowers to Jenna and press my body against Brendan's for just a brief moment. That's when I whisper, "At first, I was surprised too. Then I realized they're our family. Of course, they figured out a way to be here for you"

"For us." That's when Brendan causes the minister to exclaim, "This is extremely out of order!" Because he yanks me to him and kisses me well before we say, "I do."

Though we do get around to that.

Eventually.

CHAPTER FORTY-ONE

Danielle

PRESENT DAY

SCREAMS AND SCREECHES ARE RINGING OUT APLENTY WHILE Brendan has been holding me and I quietly reflect on the last twenty years.

Emily, Jake, Cassidy and her husband and a parade of children are all pleading with Corinna to get in the kitchen. Corinna's husband can't be heard over the racket, but Corinna's shout of, "If you want me to cook, someone had better be prepared to help!" easily is.

I'm snickering. "Poor Cori. She can't catch a break, even on vacation."

Brendan is sweating bullets. "I'm safe down here, right? She can't spot me from the house?"

"All these years and you're still terrified of her ordering you around in the kitchen?"

"It was traumatic. You have no idea."

"Brendan," I say exasperatedly, "we've all seen the episode like a million times."

"Editing. They left out the parts where Cori was mean to me," he defends himself.

I open my mouth to volunteer Brendan to be Corinna's sous chef when he topples me to the sand. His hazel eyes glow down at me. "What have you been thinking about?"

"I've just been remembering."

"What?" His head falls forward and he peppers kisses on my exposed shoulder.

"Everything. The night you told me you loved me in this very spot."

He pauses in his ministrations to inform me, "I don't think there was a moment from the time I first stepped foot on this island—and I mean from the first time when we went to Straight Wharf—I wasn't in love with you, Danielle."

I snort. "And you kiss your children with that lying mouth? For shame."

His body covers mine. "Who is the liar, my love? If you think back, really think back, every stupid thing I did was because I was trying to protect everyone."

I run my fingers over his beard into his hair. "That might be true."

It's Brendan's turn to scoff. "I was a damn juggler. I was afraid of hurting you, worrying about the kids—"

"Fighting the ghosts of your past?" I bring up his father gently. We haven't spoken much about his birth father—megalomaniac West Moore —since the unusual bequest he made Sula endure a few years ago, not long after his passing. Even though the veil of secrecy has been lifted about Brendan, JB, and Sula being siblings, it made life rocky for all West's children for some time.

Kristoffer Wilde personally thanked Brendan for having the foresight to move his legal representation to LLF LLC. "At least the barracuda who handles that side of your business can take care this media shit storm. God, I miss Carys working for us. We've never been able to replace her."

"I'm going to tell her you called her that," Brendan taunted in return.

"Why would you do something so awful? I thought we were friends?" The twinkle in the older man's eyes belied his words.

"All the more reason to play nice, Kris," I teased from my position in Brendan's office where the three of us were meeting.

The three of us laughed.

Brendan abruptly brings me back to the present when he rolls us over and curls up so I'm sitting in his lap. "I wrote a song about him."

"Excuse me?" I'm flabbergasted.

He glares down at me. "It's your fault."

"How in the hell is it my fault you wrote a song about your father?"

"Because you told me once music is my love language."

My forehead falls against his shoulder. Words escape me. "Brendan."

His arms tighten around me, stealing my breath for just a moment before they loosen.

More voices can be heard around the pool—more of our family. I can easily pick out JB and his fiancée, Sula and her husband, our children, other's kids. More of the Freemans.

Smith and Glenda. Edolie. Josiah. My mom and dad—who volunteer to help Corinna. There's a big roar of approval from the crowd.

Family.

Our family.

All of us are bound by the very thing that sets us free.

"Did you bring it down with you?" I ask quietly.

He swallows with difficulty before nodding.

Then Brendan starts to sing. With nothing accompanying him but the crashing ocean waves, the song pours out his lingering anger, frustration, and even the small amount of love that existed for the megalomaniac. He croons, "Tell me why you let me go with no fight . . ."

The private words meant for a man who is no longer alive to hear them have tears sliding down my face so fast that I can't wipe them away. Brendan begins to sip them from my cheeks as he finishes the song against my lips. "You can't tell me no, no more."

That's when he sets me to the side. Standing, he reaches into the back pocket of his jeans and pulls out a sheet of paper and a lighter. He reaches for my hand and together we walk to the water's edge. "You said it's not that I didn't love. It's that I loved so selectively because of who my father shaped me to be."

I swallow hard. "I did. Do you remember what else I said?"

He nods. "That one day I'd be grateful for it." He looks out at the vast ocean before his face meets mine. It's twisted with agony. "I need to bury my hatred of him. I found love because of who he made me be."

"Then do it."

"Will you help me?"

I nod.

He holds out the lighter in the palm of his hand. I wait until he's unfolded the paper before igniting it. His handwritten words burn quickly. Brendan holds onto it until the very last second. The ashes scatter into the ocean and the breeze. It isn't until Brendan whispers, "Bye, Dad. I hope you finally found peace," that I know West Moore somehow left Brendan with one last gift—the gift he'd denied him since he was a little boy.

He freed him.

I close my eyes and mentally send a *thank you* upward.

When I open them, Brendan's giving me a mischievous look. That's right before he bellows, "Sure, Cori! Dani said she'll be happy to help cook."

"You fiend!" I shriek. Then I get him back. "Corinna! He's been hiding down here!"

Of course, Corinna listens to me. "Brendan Blake, get your rear end up here!"

"In a minute!" he calls back. To me, he murmurs, "I have something I have to take care of first."

When he pulls me into his body, I'm breathless. I always am as I anticipate the lightning his kiss produces. Time hasn't diminished that. Still, I cock a brow. "And that is?"

"Telling you how much I love you, Danielle Madison. Thank you for giving me another chance all those years ago."

My lashes lower just as Brendan pulls me forward and his lips capture mine.

This, right here, is our forever.

Our perfect.

Our free.

When he finally leaves me breathless, he lifts his head. "Are you ready for today?"

I kiss his jaw and whisper nostalgically, "Should I bring you a cell phone for old time's sake?"

"No, because if you do, Sula and JB will take turns texting at inappropriate times. What am I saying? They're going to be awful today." He hooks an arm around my waist.

"They were so well behaved when they were seventeen, Brendan," I admonish.

"They were a royal pain in the ass," he decrees. "I kept praying you and I were the only ones who could hear the tiny *tink tink tink* from my pocket."

"That's because Sula unmuted herself for, what? Five minutes?" I reminisce fondly as we reach the stairs. Together we begin climbing. As we pass the first landing, I spy Jenna, her husband, and children over at the garage apartment. She waves happily.

The second landing leads to the basement of the main house. I hear Beckett crooning a song—likely to his wife and children. Amazing how his story came about. Two ridiculously handsome bodyguards—Kane and Mitch—stand as sentinels outside the door. A leggy blonde emerges from the basement carrying a laptop, heading in their direction. "You two aren't going to believe what I found," she boasts gleefully.

Kane's stoic demeanor fades for a moment, adoration replacing it, before his stern countenance drops back into place. "Whose classified files did you hack this time?"

I don't hear the answer as Brendan and I climb to the next level.

At the pool level, our immediate family—including Phina—are being amused by the six Freeman siblings and their assorted spouses. All are engaged in a lively debate except for Corinna who, I note with some amusement, is eying the stairs as if she's merely waiting for Brendan's appearance to act as her sous chef when she has any number of more willing volunteers.

I'll never share this with Brendan, but it's ridiculously sexy to watch him in the kitchen, whether with Corinna, his siblings, or just our kids.

All it took was the right incentive. Most things in life do.

Just as we reach the main level, my neighbors to the south were gracious enough to rent out their home to the people waving at us. Carys Burke-Lennan, her husband, her brother Ward, and his wife, who make up Brendan's and my legal team, were thrilled to be invited for our vow renewal. Even though they weren't part of our original wedding years ago, we couldn't imagine today without them. *In large part due to the support they've given to our family in the last two years since West Moore died*, I muse.

More people who have been a part of our lives forever or who have joined it recently will be arriving later including Kristoffer Wilde and his family, Shane and Amanda Reidel, the ever-expanding Freeman clan, Brendan's band, New York Times bestselling author Kee Long and her husband, Sula's grandfather-in-law. There will be close to two hundred people at this version of our wedding, but the reality is we only cared if seven people made it.

Our sons Max and Zane, our daughter Celia, and the four adults milling about the island riding herd on our children.

We enter our home and find two of those individuals dripping water on the floor of our kitchen. Brendan stops short and crosses his arms over his chest. "Do I even want to know what you wrote, Mr. StellaNova?"

Sula's husband, Arek, sputters, "What I wrote? I didn't do anything. Ask your sister what she wrote."

Sula, whose ridiculously brilliant mind is so cunning it's almost a pleasure to watch her fence against her brother or her husband, merely smiles. "All I did was make an announcement on my blog."

"It wasn't like you told the world you planned on dancing with Beckett at this shindig," Arek roars.

She studies her nails. "Which, for the record, I do."

"Whatever."

Sula's brows arc skyward at Arek's easy dismissal. "Whatever?"

"I love you. You are the stars in my sky, Sula. You crushing on Beckett Miller isn't going to change that."

Sula beams until he bellows, "But you told the whole bloody world we were pregnant before you told your me—your husband!" Arek wraps his arms around his wife, cradling her close. "Christ, Sula, I fell into the damn pool with my laptop when I read that. I was so stunned stupid."

I bounce up and down on my toes even as JB's fiancée, Liza, howls. "He was stupid, all right. I guessed a few days ago when she couldn't keep down any food."

"Yeah, way to keep me in the loop," JB grouches.

Liza glares. "I made your sister a promise."

"I felt the same damn way as Arek."

"Thank you," comes Arek's heartfelt moan from where his face is buried against Sula's neck.

"That's why I toppled in right after him when he shouted the news at me," JB mutters as he towel dries his hair.

"I'm going to be an aunt!" I exclaim.

"B? Are you all right?" Sula queries. She presses against Arek's chest to step closer to her brother.

My head swivels and I choke up at the expression on my husband's face. No, Brendan hasn't said a word. I know the man I've loved for the past twenty years better than I possibly know myself. Years of memories are chasing each other across his face. "The last time I saw him like this, he held Zane in his arms for the first time."

Sula faces me. "And that's a good thing."

"No." Brendan's face turns away. He swallows but doesn't say anything else.

I explain what my husband can't while his emotions are careening out of control. Today with what we just remembered, letting go of West, our friends and family coming together to celebrate our love and then this newest miracle? "It's a perfect thing. "

Brendan finally gets his emotions contained enough to wrap his arms around me. "It's love. And it's everything because we're together."

Just then a cork pops. JB's opened a bottle of champagne. He quickly fills five glasses before reaching for sparkling water for his sister—who makes a face as she accepts hers. He raises his glass. "To love. To finding that person who makes it feel effortless."

"To seeing beyond the surface to the person beneath," Liza adds.

"To knowing true value comes from love," Sula proclaims before her lips are captured by her husband's.

"To finding my Moore," Arek whispers against Sula's mouth.

"To all of us finding our more," I counter. There are a bunch of cheers at that.

"To feeling being perfectly free with the only person who understands you and accepts your love." Brendan's lips curve.

"Now that's something I'll drink to." JB clinks his glass to his brother's and sister's.

We all take a quick sip, which helps alleviate the tears from falling down my cheeks.

Hours later, when Brendan's using the same words in his thank you speech to our guests, he doesn't allow us to toast at that point. He says something he's said a million times in front of more people than I can count, and each time it's precious to my heart.

"I love you, my queen."

PERFECT ASSUMPTION

For the last ten years, Angela Fahey has struggled with fears and the kind vulnerability necessary to fall in love. She's held strong to the conviction love was meant for someone else until one day something slipped.

Ward Burke, a handsome lawyer who doesn't need to work if the scandal sheets declaring him a billionaire are anything to go by, has never noticed her before now. Or so she thinks.

Who knew dropping a cup of coffee all over her grumpy boss may have been the best thing to happen to both of them?

Keep reading! **Then click here** to purchase your copy on Amazon.com!

PERFECT COMPOSITION

Want a special look into Dr. Paige Kensington and gorgeous, tattooed rock god Beckett Miller's story?

Dr. Paige Kensington has worked hard to become a woman everyone respects. She's earned her medical degree, established her practice, and did so under the scrutiny of a town that will not forget she had a baby out of wedlock.

In all that time, the name of her daughter's father has never slipped out. It wasn't to protect *him* but to give her the security she deserves.

What shocks her is the forbidden sense of longing that wells up inside when they come face-to-face.

Since he now knows.

Keep reading! **Then click here** to purchase your copy on Amazon.com!

PERFECT ORDER

Leanne Miles and her identical twin, Kylie, were inseparable growing up.

Kylie was one of the hottest new indie stars—stage name, Erzulie. And Leanne? Let's say she tinkers with computers in her New York hideaway.

Until one moment changed everything.

Now Leanne's playing a dangerous game. She's assumed her sister's identity with the intent of drawing out her killer.

She'll do anything, become anyone, to get answers, even if it means turning her back on Kane McCullough. Kane's under orders to protect rockstar Beckett Miller from "Kylie."

He doesn't know who's who. Not yet.

But he will.

Keep reading! Then **click here** to purchase your copy on Amazon.com!

* * *

FREE TO DREAM

CASSIDY FREEMAN DOESN'T BELIEVE DREAMS COME TRUE BECAUSE every night her dreams trap her in a nightmare she barely escaped as a child. She maintains rigid control over all aspects of her life, giving the illusion she's strong and confident. Allowing very few close enough to see the brave heart buried beneath, she's convinced she'll carry her burdens alone.

From the minute they met, Caleb Lockwood disrupted everything by destroying her sense of order. His patience, compassion and sensuality obliterated her defenses. It's as if he knew her from the inside out.

Helping his younger brother hire a wedding planner shouldn't have led to this. In just a few short days, Caleb's learned untold secrets about his family – and about the Freemans. When he demands to meet them, he doesn't expect the pull he feels towards the petite dynamo in front of him whom life has dealt an unspeakable hand.

With Caleb, Cassidy's lost her semblance of control. Now, she's not sure she wants it back. Not if giving it up means having a chance at something she never imagined.

Love.

Click HERE to buy on Amazon or read in KU!

FREE TO RUN

Alison Freeman met Keene Marshall because of a dare she wholeheartedly regrets accepting.

As her family's corporate lawyer, Alison discards the idea of love as quickly as she negotiates contracts. Brutally. She realizes she's been a fool over Keene—who is now intimately embedded in her family. It only adds to the enormity of emotions churning inside about her life.

Keene Marshall is arrogant enough to know his time with Alison left a lasting impression. He has yet to determine what place she's going to hold in his life, but he knows there will be one. They burn too hot for there not to be.

Having closed himself off from his humanity for so long, finding Alison again presents its own set of challenges. Keene struggles with everything from his family to the walls Alison persistently builds between them. And he can't handle the emotions that come with being denied what he wants.

Alison's wary of Keene. Something is holding her back, except every time his lips touch hers, she's flung into the race of her life for the one thing she claims she never wanted to win.

Click HERE to buy on Amazon or read in KU!

FREE TO REJOICE

Dr. Jason Ross has an unprecedented week off during the holiday season to spend with his husband and family. Anticipating his greatest challenge will be keeping his husband's gift buying under control, he's excited for the week ahead.

But life doesn't take a vacation even when doctors want to.

Reality destroys Jason's yuletide cheer leaving him as twisted as some of his family's holiday traditions. Will it take a miracle for Jason to find joy in the holidays?

Or does Jason just need love?

Click HERE to buy on Amazon or read in KU!

FREE TO BREATHE

Baker Corinna Freeman cut all ties with Colby Hunt when she learned what the handsome military officer really thought about her and her cooking skills. She walked away; heartbroken, pride in tatters, keeping secrets she was far too young to shoulder.

Now, a decade later, Corinna's reputation is legendary — both in and out of the kitchen. This bold woman is determined to live life to its fullest while she can.

There's just one major problem...

Colby's suddenly turning up everywhere acting as if nothing has changed between them in the last ten years. It infuriates her because he can still stir her up.

Colby Hunt never understood why Corinna walked out of his life without a word. He's not letting this chance pass to figure out what happened with the voluptuous beauty who captured his heart. Despite his anger, he's never really let her go.

But there's something she's hiding...

Unlike Corinna's perfect cakes, secrets fall apart. When they do, they will test the strength and courage of not only Corinna and Colby but the entire Freeman family.

Click HERE to buy on Amazon or read in KU!

FREE TO BELIEVE

In the wake of a broken engagement, Emily Freeman is left to sew together the pieces of her life. A single phone call changes her future from bleak acceptance to overwhelming opportunity.

Her family can't help her find her artistic spirit — something she needs now more than ever. Desperate for rejuvenation, Em goes on a journey to find herself.

Only she finds so much more...

Jacob Madison has never regretted walking away from pursuing music professionally since the moment his daughter was put in his arms. Jake needs time to get back on an even beat with her now that she's a teenager. But soon he finds himself face-to-face with a woman who stirs fires deep inside despite her icy demeanor.

Nothing is what it seems...

For Em to achieve her wildest dreams, she'll have to conquer her two biggest fears — love and death. And she'll have to do both while protecting those she loves from the hardest thing imaginable.

Herself.

Click HERE to buy on Amazon or read in KU!

FREE TO LIVE

Wedding photographer Holly Freeman holds her camera up to act as a mask; blocking the world from seeing the vulnerability she never quite let go of. She still feels she owes a debt for the second chance at life she's more than repaid.

One perfect shot...

Firefighter Joseph Bianco lost love in a way that left deep emotional wounds. There's no place for a personal life between the fires he fights every day and the bitterness he holds back at night.

Scars heal...

As their worlds collide, they want nothing more than friendship. But it's not long before Holly and Joe both realize they are not truly living despite the lies they tell themselves.

Will these friends-to-lovers be able to battle their pasts to find the love they deserve?

Click HERE to buy on Amazon or read in KU!

FREE TO DANCE

JUST DANCE

Marco Houde's world revolves around the impossibly alluring nightclub built on the outskirts of Manhattan. Even as the wealthy and elite line up night after night for entry, there's a part of him few manage to touch.

Then he watched her saunter into Redemption. Fireworks went off inside him.

Brilliant financier Lynne Bradbury is determined to give her best friend the bachelorette party of her dreams. Along with the rambunctious Freeman clan, she ends up moving and shaking in the VIP section. But it isn't long before she accuses him of being a bad liar for treating her differently than he does the others.

She just doesn't understand why.

As the music plays, Lynne can't quite shake off the feeling there's more to Marco than meets the eye, especially after he whirls her around the dance floor.

Because that one dance between them changes everything.

Click HERE to buy on Amazon or read in KU!

FREE TO WISH

WISH UPON THE RIGHT STAR

Known as the face for Amaryllis Events, Jenna Madison is a familiar sight on social media platforms around the globe. Even before she met her soon-to-be stepmother—renowned fashion designer, Emily Freeman —Jenna made a pact with herself to make a difference in the world of fashion. She didn't realize how much she'd have to endure along the way to achieve success.

In the five years since Jenna graduated college, she still can't forget the last day of her international marketing class. After all, despite the spark that arced between them, Professor Finn O'Roarke pushed her away after he finished ravishing her body.

And her heart.

Finn has spent the last five years mourning the loss of Jenna from his life. When granted his wish to speak with Jenna, he doesn't know how to convince her of his intentions. He has one chance to repair the damage he's wrought.

As for Jenna, can she relinquish the past? Or will she be left forever wishing for love based on respect, trust, and faith?

**EXPANDED FROM THE ORIGINAL
1,001 DARK NIGHTS SHORT STORY WINNER**

Click HERE to buy from Amazon or read in KU!

FREE TO PROTECT

CAPTAIN BRETT STEWART IS A SECOND-GENERATION FIREFIGHTER. His life is irrevocably changed when he enters a burning building only to be trapped. Now, recovered from his injuries, he's eager to don the gear that failed him and get back to work.

He never expects his blood to ignite when he sees a swoosh of gray across a crowded fundraiser.

He has to meet her.

Local business owner Jillian Beale knows all too well fire can destroy everything in its wake. From a childhood of uncertainty, she was content until her safety net incinerated one afternoon. Then she has no choice but to fight to protect her future.

But after Brett leads her out onto the dance floor, her vision for the future goes up in smoke.

After all, who better than she knows that touching fire burns?

Click HERE to buy on Amazon or read in KU!

FREE TO REUNITE

You have been cordially invited to a night of secrets. Cravings and longings can no longer be denied.

At least that's what the invitation should have said.

Kelsey Kennedy attended her fifteen-year reunion against her better judgment. Maybe if she showed the varmints she went to school with how her appearance changed, she'd finally have her vengeance.

Decking herself out for the event, Kelsey's no longer stuck hiding her body in value pack clothes. A single confrontation changes her mind on stepping through the doors. Deciding to bail on the reunion at the last second, the only evidence she's been at the affair is the name tag bearing her hated nickname—King Kong.

Keyed up with emotion, Kelsey heads for the hotel bar, where she comes face-to-face with Benedict Perrault, the boy she loved. Her final ruin. The boy she never got over. Willfully, she uses the fact he doesn't recognize her for one fiery night in his bed.

Benedict doesn't put together the woman at the bar with the one he was intent to make amends with. Everything crashes down all at once when he realizes the truth. Kelsey is no longer the overweight girl who needs his protection. She's built a life of her own.

And he's determined to find out who she is beneath the façade she portrays.

Will they be free to reunite their past with their present, or will the shadows keep them apart until the next post about a high school reunion?

Click HERE to buy on Amazon or read in KU!

ACKNOWLEDGMENTS

Nathan, thank you for holding on exactly the way I've always needed you to. I love you.

To my son, I *always* love you more.

Mom, I hope you adore the scene I wrote with you in mind. Love you! XOXO

Jen, I love you, but go argue with Linda. I know you licked the cover first.

My Meows, always. Forever. And, for the first time, we're together on release day!

To the Delta Kappa Epsilons of my past, my other "brothers." You were on my mind, as were the many times I spent looking at the photos on the ΔKE house walls.

Amy, Kristin, and Dawn, you three women are brilliant, strong, and an unbelievable part of my life. Thank you! XOXO

To Missy Borucki, thank you for always pushing me for more. XOXO.

To Holly Malgieri, my twin and fellow Yankees fan. I knew you would love that scene when you read it. I love you!

To photographer Wander Aguiar, Andrey Bahia, Jenny Flores, and Donna Lathan, I have fully recovered from my sprained ankle, which is what occurred when I tripped after seeing Robbin's photo! LOL

To my cover designer, Deborah Bradseth, this cover sings. It's everything. XOXO

To Gel, at Tempting Illustrations, incredible beauty!

To the team at Foreword PR, thank you for everything, every day. From the first Amaryllis book to now, I can't stop thanking you enough.

Linda Russell, you have to *share* with Jen this time. Share. Just share. I love you. Thank you for EVERYTHING you've done up to this release.

Finally, to you, my readers, Brendan and Danielle's story happened because of your love of their characters.

I am overwhelmed by your comments and reviews. I love hearing from every one of you. Thank you for your support and for choosing to read my words.

ABOUT THE AUTHOR

Tracey Jerald knew she was meant to be a writer when she would re-write the ending of books in her head on her bike when she was a young girl growing up in southern Connecticut. It wasn't long before she was typing alternate endings and extended epilogues "just for fun".

After college in Florida, where she obtained a degree in Criminal Justice swearing she saw things she'll never quite believe and never quite forget, Tracey traded the world of law and order for IT. Her work for a world-wide internet startup transferred her to Northern Virginia where she met her husband in what many call their own happily ever after. They have one son.

When she's not busy with her family or writing, Tracey can be found in her home in north Florida drinking coffee, reading, training for a runDisney event, or feeding her addiction to HGTV.

To follow Tracey, go to her website at *https://www.traceyjerald.com*.

www.ingramcontent.com/pod-product-compliance
Lightning Source LLC
Chambersburg PA
CBHW071425260626
47170CB00008B/2601